"You taste like honey...."

Michael's mouth dampened Ashley's as he spoke, his kiss gentle but insistent until her lips parted to admit him. God, she was sexy!

A breathy sigh escaped Ashley's throat, becoming lost in Michael's. His hand rested on her waist and she grasped his arms to steady herself against the weakness spreading through her body. His relentless seeking continued until he explored every secret her mouth offered, and then he silently urged her to learn his . . . just as intimately.

Her tongue slipped in and found his taste, sweet and drugging. The latent passion that had been building for days between them flared quickly, sweeping them into a spiral.

Suddenly, her prudent career-woman self resurfaced to issue a warning—she was about to commit occupational suicide. She dragged her mouth from his. "We can't . . . I don't want . . ."

"You don't want— Hey, sweetheart, then you're sending the wrong signals."

Michael's mouth claimed hers again, bent on exposing the futility of her protest.

Kate Jenkins has always been fascinated by the eccentricities of Southern families—in particular, by the "terminally single" lives of maiden aunts. She toyed with the idea of writing about such a woman as she accompanied her husband on several job transfers across the U.S. In Minneapolis, Kate took a temporary office job. When a team of auditors descended on the company, she became curious about the effects of their nomadic lives on their personal lives. Out of the melding of those two notions emerged *Terminally Single*. Enjoy!

Books by Kate Jenkins

Terminally Single

KATE JENKINS

Harlequin Books

TORONTO • NEW YORK • LONDON
AMSTERDAM • PARIS • SYDNEY • HAMBURG
STOCKHOLM • ATHENS • TOKYO • MILAN

To my editor, Valerie Hayward,
for her daring rescue mission.
And to Janece,
the kind of friend every writer needs

Published April 1991

ISBN 0-373-25443-1

TERMINALLY SINGLE

I KNEW I SHOULDN'T have gotten up this morning.

That fleeting thought flashed through Ashley Atwood's head at the moment of impact. Then the sound of shattering glass and crumpling metal drove everything else from her mind. Flung forward by the force of the collision, she gasped when the seat belt snapped against her collarbone and across her stomach.

She'd heard that just before death, your entire life flashed before your eyes. Her time must not be up yet, because her only vision was of paperwork—reams of rental-car insurance forms and company reports.

After a few seconds of listening to the annoying slap-squeak of windshield wipers, she loosened her two-handed death grip on the steering wheel and took an inventory of her moving parts. Satisfied when everything functioned on command, she glanced in the rearview mirror.

An overnight-package delivery van had jumped onto the rear bumper of her rented sedan, and then kept on going, pleating her trunk lid like a homemade paper fan. As if this mess wasn't all *his* fault, that lunatic of a driver was irately honking at her!

Ashley forgot about the violent April thunderstorm that was drenching Minneapolis, forgot she was due to start a new assignment in only minutes, forgot her accountant's outfit and demeanor. From her handbag she pulled out a clear plastic shower cap, courtesy of the hotel, and stuffed as much of her hair as would fit under it. Like a warrior arming for battle, she rearranged the transparent dry-cleaner's bag she had put on to serve as a makeshift raincoat, and wrenched open the door. Muttering curses at the crazed honker, she swiveled sideways and scrambled from her car—only to step into ankle-deep water.

Yes. It was definitely one of those days.

The delivery driver rolled out of his van and slogged toward her. He wore a heavy yellow slicker, hood and rubber boots, while her flimsy protection whipped noisily in the gale-force gusts.

In jarring contrast to his monstrous size was his angelic baby face, which didn't look a day over fourteen. His fury was colossal.

"What the hell were you trying to do, lady?"

She jerked her head up and stiffened her shoulders. So it was a confrontation he wanted. No problem. She was incensed enough to give him a good one. "Why, I wasn't *trying* to do anything," she said, drawing out the sarcasm with her oozing-honey accent. "I was driving slowly and carefully in a flooded parking lot. Until you—"

"Now, wait just a minute!"

"No. *You* wait!" She planted both hands on her hips, attempting to ignore the chilly rain soaking through the sleeves of her taupe silk suit. If she could have worn the cleaner's bag like a straightjacket, it might have done a somewhat better job of keeping her dry. However, since she'd had to tear arm slits so she could drive, she was getting drenched. "Let me refresh your memory. You hit me, buddy."

He stepped closer and glowered down at her. "You were in my way, creeping along like a snail, holding me up. I have deadlines to make. What was I supposed to do?"

"Run over me, so it seems." Intimidation was tricky when your opponent towered over you by at least a foot. "I had no idea that driving cautiously in heavy rain gave you the green light to rear-end me. I'll have to check with—" she paused to enunciate the name on his van before finishing "—and see if that's company policy."

The man blinked twice and opened his mouth, then shook his head. "Are you crazy, lady?"

Ashley's temper flared. "I'm perfectly sane, fella. Barreling through here on slick roads, however, suggests maniacal tendencies on your part."

"That does it," he roared, furiously advancing on her.

"Resorting to force, are we?" Ashley threw up both hands in what she hoped was a reasonable facsimile of a karate stance. She recalled you were supposed to accompany the crouch with some sort of shout, then decided that might be overkill. "Come on, buster. Take one more step."

"What's the trouble?" a calm male voice asked from behind her.

"Nothing I can't handle," she assured the unseen stranger as she blew at a curl dangling in front of her right eye. "Stand back. When I take him down, this puppy's going to splash like Shamu."

Michael Jordan clamped his teeth together to keep from laughing aloud. He hadn't stopped with the intention of getting involved in a parking-lot brawl. The fender bender was blocking his entrance to the underground garage and he'd gotten out of his car to ask if they would move their vehicles forward enough for him to get past. He recognized that the tall figure in rain gear was Scott. Scott daily delivered an overnight pack from the company's home office. That was normal. Seeing Scott backing away from a petite challenger poised to attack was a humorous break in routine. The shower cap and see-through laundry bag she was wearing added to the comedy of the confrontation.

"What's the matter, peanut?" she taunted. "Afraid to risk it?"

Michael cleared his throat and edged between the two combatants. "What happened, Scott?"

"What happened?" the woman demanded incredulously, poking several tendrils of dark-honey-colored hair back under the shower cap with one hand while gesturing at the wreckage with her other. "Isn't it obvious? That bozo ran into me. From behind. Now he has the nerve to claim that I'm responsible. Talk about a sauce brain!"

"Why, you—"

"Look, this isn't accomplishing anything," Michael interrupted. He needed the driveway cleared so he could get to work. He was already late, and that damned internal auditor would be waiting to pounce on him. "If you'll both cool off, we can settle this without name-calling."

"Mr. Jordan, I can explain," Scott offered, suddenly meek.

Ashley looked at their arbitrator a split second before his name registered. Then she groaned, wondering what else could happen to compound her misery. Jordan was a fairly common name. Was it too much to hope that there might be more than one Jordan working in this particular building? "*Michael* Jordan?" she ventured.

Puzzled, he nodded.

"Vice president, computer division of—?"

"WTS." He completed her query, naming the electronics conglomerate they both worked for.

"I might have known," Ashley said ruefully, glaring at her shins where a pair of runs had creeped up like cheap underwear. The day was quickly going from bad to horrendous. Still, there was nothing to do except take a stab at salvaging her dignity. One thing she knew about Michael Jordan was that he had started out in accounting. Maybe he could stir up a little empathy for a fellow bean-counter.

Water began trickling down her neck to form chilly pools inside her collar as she smiled and extended her hand. "I'm Ashley Atwood, your internal auditor. We have an eight o'clock appointment."

ASHLEY HAD NO PATIENCE with women who expected a man to rescue them from all of life's trials. However, this time she was grateful that Michael had insisted on taking over. Assuring her he would resolve everything, he guided her toward his battered Land Rover to wait out of the rain, while he straightened things out with Scott. Afterward he'd drive her back to the hotel to change clothes. She had started to protest that she could handle it herself, but was relieved when he assured her he was glad to help her out. She wasn't feeling too capable and confident at the moment.

Michael Jordan was both capable and confident. Otherwise he wouldn't have the job he had.

She reached for the door handle and gaped at how high she'd have to step to get in. At five-three, she hadn't been blessed with the world's longest legs. Her narrow skirt had only a modest vent in the front, and she could already hear stitches ripping if she tried to mount this beast. Oh, well, what did she have to lose? The outfit was already trashed.

Forsaking modesty, Ashley tossed her briefcase onto the floorboard, hiked her skirt above her knees and clambered up. She sighed and peeled off the sodden shower cap, cramming it into a hanging litter bag.

Next time I wake up and it's storming, I swear I'm going to smash the alarm and stay in bed, she told herself. After a couple of futile attempts to revive her drooping, tangled curls with her fingers, she gave up and looked at the clutter surrounding her. Boxes and bags filled the rear seat. A stack of canvases and an assortment of sporting goods took up the remaining space. This ancient, messy vehicle didn't fit the image of a man in Michael's position. Conforming to type had been a problem for Ashley all her life. She knew all about the strain of maintaining deceptive appearances—in her profession, and especially within her family.

She studied the two men talking a few feet away, and this time it wasn't the yellow-clad monster that commanded her attention. Although he stood several inches shorter than Scott, Michael's lithe and lean six-foot frame wasn't concealed by his casually-worn trench coat. And if his choice of vehicle was unconventional, his conservative, navy-blue suit and striped silk tie were the standard executive's uniform.

Ashley had expected him to be older, more reserved, and not quite so attractive. Sharp, competent, aggressive, yes. But in the three years she'd spent doing internal audits at various branch offices, she had rarely encountered a corporate executive that had intrigued her on a personal level.

"Oh, lordy," she whispered, and closed her eyes. It was going to be a long haul unless she got that kind of notion out of her head. The implications were so disturbing that she refused to consider them.

By the time Michael jumped in and cranked the motor, she had instructed herself to keep him at a professional distance. "Do you think the rental-car people are going to string me up?" she asked him.

He chuckled. "I'll make a couple of phone calls from your hotel and see what I can do. With any luck, you'll live to drive again."

When he stripped the gears in starting off, Ashley gritted her teeth. "I really didn't expect limo service."

He smiled at her wry comment and gave the dashboard an affectionate pat. "Isn't she a beauty? I couldn't get along without Agnes."

"This thing is named Agnes?"

"Right. After the lady who sold her to me. Hang on. High water ahead."

Twin geysers shot up as "Agnes" plowed through a series of deep puddles in one corner of the parking lot, then was aggressively nosed by Michael into the flow of street traffic. Ashley clung to her armrest with fingers still shaky from the recent accident. "I suppose you need something durable like a Land Rover in this climate."

"Don't tell me you're one of those women who's only impressed by status cars," he said disdainfully. "As far as I'm concerned, everybody else on the face of the earth can drive a Saab turbo. If one more person tries to sell me on the wonders of owning one, I won't be accountable for my actions."

"You'll not hear that lecture from me. I'm still driving the first car I ever had." She smiled at the modest description of her classic MG.

"Now that I can understand." He switched off the radio talk-show droning in the background. "About the parking lot scene—how far advanced are you in karate?"

"Well, I don't like to brag," she said smugly, "but I know practically everything you can learn from watching one Bruce Lee movie." She laughed with him, certain he'd already diagnosed her as deranged for threatening the massive Scott. "What can I say?

Sometimes I'm impulsive." *Like now, when I shouldn't have admitted that to you.*

He let her confession pass, and shifted his attention to her voice. "I like your accent."

Ashley nodded, accustomed to similar remarks. "One thing that's guaranteed to cause comment in the North is a Southern accent."

"Where are you from?"

She told him, eliding the *r* so it sounded like Challston. "South Carolina. I live in Atlanta now— at least for the few days a month that I'm home."

"My family moved to Atlanta when I was twelve and I promptly fell victim to the girl next door. Every time she drawled 'Michael, Ah declare,' I became putty in her hands."

"She still practicing her Southern wiles on you?" Ashley asked, attempting to sound nonchalant. Her teeth clenched at the thought of him married to the girl next door—or anyone else. Not a good sign.

"Hardly. We moved away after two years and she went on to become a debutante. I doubt if we turned out to be each other's type." He pumped the brakes to slow for a light. "You could pass for the type. A debutante, I mean."

She flinched, then quickly camouflaged her reaction. He had no way of knowing about the family battle that had erupted when she'd refused to come out, pronouncing the ritual a silly, indulgent extravagance. "Why would you even think such a thing?"

"No offense intended, if you're into stuff like that. It's just my impression that a deb's expectations are sort of misguided."

"You got that right," she agreed vehemently.

"Must be rough having a job that keeps you on the road all the time. I'd get tired of living out of a suitcase pretty fast."

Michael had noticed how distant and uncompromising her voice sounded. He adroitly moved on to another topic.

"It's not as grim as some traveling jobs. I'm usually in one place for a month to six weeks, and we stay in suites instead of just a hotel room. It isn't so bad."

"Still, it must put a crater in your social life."

She hesitated before replying. "Itinerant accountants are better off without encumbrances." In reality, the job was ideal for someone fated to be terminally single—someone like herself. It was the main reason she'd signed a second two-year contract.

Michael looked intently at her, as if he were seeing her for the first time. "You have very unusual eyes. Do they run in the family?"

"No, except for Aunt Kitty and me. I must have inherited them from her." Ashley's legacy from Katherine Atwood transcended physical characteristics. It charted the course of her life. Everything she'd done for the past ten years represented a conscious decision to follow Kitty's example. Like Kitty, Great-Aunt Fan and other Atwood women before them, Ashley believed she was destined to be a maiden aunt. That certainty was as deeply ingrained in her as the Atwood family was in Charleston. Centuries of tradition were indisputably powerful motivators.

"They're the same shade of gray as Spanish moss," Michael observed, drawing her back to the present. "I never paint portraits, but it would be a real challenge to get that color just right."

"An accountant who paints?"

He wasn't surprised that she would know something about his background. "I dabble. For fun." His attention alternated between driving and glancing into her eyes.

After what she'd been through earlier, Michael's lack of concentration on the traffic bothered her. Or was it the penetrating brown eyes of the too-handsome stranger that made her uneasy?

"Would you mind watching the road?" Ashley suggested in a tone she hoped would seem tactful rather than panicked. "My eyes are green, not gray. It says so on my driver's license."

Michael took one last look before focusing straight ahead, giving her the opportunity to study him more closely, In profile, his features were classically sculpted—a sharply defined jawline, narrow nose, full, curved lips. His dark brown hair had survived the battle with the elements far better than her own. It skimmed the tops of his ears and swept over his forehead from a side part. Would his chest—?

What was going on? She was here to scrutinize the man's business practices, not to scout him as a potential centerfold. Ashley looked out the side window, blindly focusing on the cars in the next lane. Her eyes kept gravitating back to Michael. His hands were wrapped around the steering wheel. His fingers were long and agile, intimating that he was skillful, artistic, sensitive. And sensual.

These delusions were getting out of control. Had she cracked her head on the windshield or something?

"What about the name?"

"Pardon?" His conversational shifts plus his mystifying appeal were making her edgy.

He raised one index finger. "Let me guess. Your mother saw *Gone With the Wind*, fell in love with Leslie Howard and vowed to name her firstborn Ashley."

"You're way off base there." The idea of naming a child after a movie character would strike Eleanor Atwood as too common for words. "Now that you mention it, naming us was probably the most whimsical thing Mother's ever done."

"Us?"

She should have kept her mouth shut. He'd zeroed right in on the critical word. "My sister and I. Ashley and Cooper, after the two rivers that meet in Charleston to 'form' the Atlantic Ocean."

He ignored her feeble joke and asked, "Is your sister impulsive, too?"

"Are you kidding? Nothing like this morning's escapade would dare happen to Cooper. She calculates every move from beginning to end, and everything turns out precisely as planned." Unlike her older sister, Ashley, Cooper always, *always*, did the proper thing at the right time.

"Predictable and perfect. Boring!"

Ashley murmured in agreement, feeling easier since they had just reached her hotel. Michael was a little too observant, too perceptive, too everything for her peace of mind. She welcomed the excuse to escape and regroup.

Thank heaven she'd finally learned to pack an emergency bag with several days' necessities and carry it on the plane with her. Once she changed into a dry suit and high-necked blouse, got her hair subdued, her working persona would emerge on cue. Ashley Atwood, the superefficient accountant, wouldn't let anyone or anything distract her.

Michael's muscular, dark, good looks, his straightforward charm and professional accomplishments qualified him as female daydream material.

Forget the daydreams. She wasn't in the market for any kind of man.

WHAT A WASTE, Michael reflected, frowning, as he observed Ashley's confident march from the elevator. During the twenty minutes since she'd left him in the lobby, she had transformed herself into a dressed-for-success clone. Her naturally curly hair was twisted into a knot, pulled back so tightly she would probably get the headache she deserved. The prim little suit looked expensive, but its bland color reminded him of oatmeal. He'd rather see her in something red and sassy, more in keeping with his original impression of her.

It was bad enough that men had to wear the same monotonous uniform day after day. Equality in the workplace aside, he didn't understand why career women felt compelled to dress like their male counterparts.

He didn't like to make the comparison; still, Ashley's attire and her profession conjured up unpleasant reminders of his mother's recent transformation. Since she'd gone back to college and gotten her accounting degree, Bettina Jordan had turned into an older version of the woman approaching him now. Locked on target. All business. Inaccessible.

Evidently all men didn't share his opinion of women in suits. Scanning the lobby, he saw several admiring male gazes directed at Ashley. Although their approving looks were obvious, he couldn't fault their taste. Even tightly buttoned-up in business garb, she was an eye-catcher.

Ashley wasn't beautiful in the classic sense, which was precisely why Michael had been intrigued from the moment he saw her. Traditional beauty had never interested him much. *Exotic* didn't quite describe Ashley. It came close, though.

Michael was a sucker for eyes, especially if they were a distinctive shape and color. She'd insisted hers were green. If so, they were shadowed with enough gray to banish any hint of emerald. Her complexion was the olive tone usually found combined with dark hair and eyes. She wasn't very tall. Her charm-school-perfect posture gave her maximum benefit from every inch. Wrapped in flapping plastic and crouched to attack, Ashley Atwood had acted invincible. He replayed the earlier scene and grinned.

He was also a sucker for women who had spirit enough to indulge their outrageous whims. Like giant-baiting in a downpour.

His frown deepened. This new Ashley had discarded her rashness along with the innovative rainwear. The smile she wore, like her outfit, labeled her cool and remote. He'd bet she thought her mouth was too wide, that her lower lip was pouty and too full to match the upper one. She would have been right— and, God, he was already hungry for the taste of those lips.

"Is my lipstick smeared or something?"

She'd caught him staring at her mouth. He was no better than those lobby lotharios who'd been ogling her. "Your lip . . . stick is fine." To cover his gaffe, he rattled off the details of how he'd arranged to have the wrecked car exchanged for a replacement before five o'clock. "I also reported it to the insurance company, so you won't have to bother with that."

Ashley shivered, certain the chill was more than a delayed reaction to her soaking. Not only had Michael taken over, he'd done it too easily and expertly for her comfort. "I counted on being snarled in red tape for an eternity. How did you cut through it?"

He guided her toward the door. "Pipelines to the right people. The trick is knowing who to call to get your problem solved."

"I'll have to remember that," she said, wishing his hand cupping her elbow didn't feel so warm, so right.

They'd parked under the covered driveway, so Ashley had decided to forgo her dry-cleaning bag creation. She could share Michael's umbrella to avoid getting waterlogged again. "Thanks for all you've done," she said after he helped her into Agnes. "I owe you one."

"It'll be a pleasure to collect."

Their gazes meshed for a few seconds while, for Ashley, the word *pleasure* took on a whole range of electrifying meanings. Her mouth went dry. *Another bad sign. No, not bad. Disastrous.* She laced her fingers together, reminding herself that Ashley Atwood did not go all slushy inside because a good-looking man knew his way around a double entendre. Believing she was immune to that sort of nonsense didn't halt the burgeoning warmth inside her.

The office wasn't far from her hotel and Ashley managed to regain her equilibrium during the drive back. Her initial attraction to Michael was a lapse, a momentary weakness, most likely caused by the accident. It wouldn't happen again.

When they reached their building, he inserted a plastic card in a slot and an automatic door rose to admit them into an underground garage. "Rank has its privileges," he explained when she commented that it was too bad some people had to park and walk in the rain. Pulling into an assigned space, he removed the car keys and twirled them on his forefinger.

"There's a cafeteria on the basement level, so you won't have to go out at noon." His slow reappraisal of her should have been insulting. It wasn't, and she couldn't figure out why. "On second thought, you probably skip a few meals. Not much excess fat on those bones."

Ashley fumbled with her briefcase and groped for the passenger door handle, blaming the accident for her clumsiness. "Breakfast is expendable. Dinner, negotiable. Lunch is mandatory. I'm the world's biggest grouch without it."

"In that case, we'll go together. Is one okay?"

Instinct told her to make a polite excuse—not to spend more time with him than was absolutely necessary. If she refused, she'd be admitting that there was a bond between them, beyond their professional one. She often shared meals with company personnel in branch offices. It was acceptable and appropriate under the circumstances. Just business. Michael Jordan was no different from any other employee.

"One o'clock is fine," she said decisively, walking with him toward the elevator.

Their company occupied the building's entire top floor. Private offices lined the exterior walls while the open, inner area was filled with desks and file cabinets, arranged to separate the various departments. Michael's office was at one end, in a corner, with a glass-walled conference room on each side. During the past three years, Ashley had seen essentially the same configuration in more than ten cities. She also knew her audit team would be assigned to one of the conference rooms. Over the next few weeks, she'd have to work quite literally side by side with Michael Jordan.

He ushered her into a room that overlooked a landscaped greenbelt whose row of maple saplings was bent low by the heavy downpour. Beyond was a small lake, its murky surface swirling with waves.

Ashley deposited her briefcase on a table and squared her shoulders for the grand tour. This was what she did best. She was in her element. So why was her stomach impersonating a jumping bean? It was barely nine o'clock and this had been one of the most unsettling days she could recall. Time to get herself back on track.

Michael introduced her to Claudia Garrett, his administrative assistant, explaining that Claudia could help her find any information and materials she needed.

"What he means," the tall, athletic-looking blonde added, "is that I've done time on just about every job in this joint." She grinned at Ashley, as if they were co-conspirators. "Of course, now that I've clawed my way to the top, I get to tell everyone else what to do." She directed the grin at her boss before amending, "Almost everyone."

Ashley knew at once that while Michael didn't rule by intimidation, there was no confusion about who ran the show.

When he took her to meet the departmental supervisors, they all greeted her politely, assuring her of their willingness to cooperate. Ashley wasn't usually paranoid; nevertheless, she couldn't shake the feeling that everyone began talking about her as soon as she walked away.

By the time they'd made the circuit and returned to the conference room, she couldn't wait to get started. Surely that would chase away all the unsettling vibrations she felt when Michael was anywhere in the vicinity. She draped her jacket over an empty chairback, then took out her calculator. Next came a stack of pads, rulers and the special mechanical pencil and eraser which she arranged around her in a precise pattern.

"Looks like I'm being dismissed," Michael said from the doorway. "Let me know if you need anything else. Otherwise, I'll see you at one."

Ashley began shuffling a pile of papers so she didn't have to look at him. "Thanks again for everything."

"No problem." He turned and started toward his office, but stuck his head back around the doorframe to add, "By the way, I'm glad you're here."

Just when she'd started feeling calmer, his comment rattled her almost as much as those perceptive brown eyes and his conspiratorial smile. "That's not the reception I usually get when I descend to do an internal audit."

"Who's talking about the audit?"

2

WHEN REVIEWING RECORDS and operations for a company, Ashley employed an audit program written by herself. After three years' experience with it, she could easily adapt the program to any area or function selected for examination. This morning's delay had thrown her off stride. Her mind kept straying back to Michael Jordan. She'd only met him a couple of hours ago, but somehow he'd gotten to her.

Ashley was keenly aware of his presence in the adjoining room. Several times during the morning she had looked out through the glass walls and spotted Michael talking to some of his employees. Invariably their eyes would meet, then she'd quickly pretend absorption in her work. More than once, she'd run a tape of meaningless calculations in order to look busy.

By lunchtime her stomach was rebelling audibly— whether from hunger or expectancy, she wasn't quite sure. When she and Michael entered the cafeteria after one, Ashley noticed they received more than a few curious glances. In her experience, a visiting auditor having lunch with the boss had seldom generated so much attention.

A satisfying meal was all she needed to get rid of the lingering uneasiness. She ordered the soup-and-sandwich special. Still, those looks were hard to ignore. "Why all the interest because we're eating lunch together?" she asked when Michael plunked his tray on their table.

He shrugged, surveying the room. "Probably because I don't eat here often. When I do, it's never with someone from work."

"Never?"

"Nope. I get along with everyone, but I don't socialize with them at all, not even for lunch." He dug into a generous serving of lasagna.

"I hope you don't feel obligated to baby-sit me. I've eaten alone enough that it doesn't bother me." Brave words, when in fact solitary meals were one of the things she dreaded most.

"Back up a step. I promise you, baby-sitting is not one of my talents. I wanted to spend some time with you, so I asked. A simple invitation." He watched her startled reaction. "Just like this one. How about dinner?"

Auditors couldn't indulge in such temptations. "I'm sorry, I can't."

He studied her. "Guess you have a patented excuse for discouraging men who move too fast."

Before today, I never needed one. Ashley stared at her ham-and-cheese sandwich, grateful to have an easy way out. "The rest of my audit team gets in to-night and I'm picking them up at the airport."

"What time's their plane due?"

"Nine-thirty, if we're lucky. With this weather, I suppose it'll be late." Like eating alone, delayed flights were another consequence of her transient life-style. Considering the alternative, both were reasonable prices to pay.

"Listen, if our airport can operate during blizzards, I don't think this little storm is anything to worry about." Michael put down his fork. "Why don't I pick you up for dinner and then take you out there? That way, you won't have to drive."

"I can look after myself. You don't have—"

"Ashley, either your ears aren't working or you're uncommonly stubborn. Since when does inviting you to share a meal mean you can't take care of yourself? Are you always so defensive?"

"No, not really." Rarely did she feel it necessary to be this guarded. Michael had put her senses on red alert.

"Hey, I'm harmless," he said with a disarming grin.

She dropped her sandwich and squinted across the table. "I expect your nose to start growing after a whopper like that." His disarming smile evolved into full-fledged laughing. Meaning, she had to get them onto a serious basis again. "I appreciate the offer of dinner. I think we'd better confine our association to the office. I'm here to audit you, to examine how you manage the computer-operations division. How would it look if we were seen together after hours?"

"In the first place, I don't give a damn how it looks," Michael replied brusquely, lowering his voice when several spectators gave up the pretense of eating to eavesdrop. "When I walk out the door at night, the job no longer owns me. What I—we do on our off time is nobody's business."

"All the same," she argued, knowing she was losing ground, "your rule about socializing with people from the company should apply to me, too. I don't expect to be entertained because I'm from out of town."

He shoved aside the empty plate and planted his elbows on the table. "You're wasting time with excuses. The only valid one is that you don't like me. Say so, and I'll leave you alone."

She had trouble swallowing her sandwich. It was almost as difficult as meeting his eyes. Ashley couldn't lie, even as a means of self-protection.

"Is that the reason you keep putting up roadblocks? You can't stand the thought of being with me?"

Ashley's vagabond work-life ruled out serious relationships or even dating. She was friends with a group of unattached men and women who regularly went out together. She wasn't accustomed to being with a man who was this personal or this persistent.

"No," she replied with visible discomfort. "I suppose I could regard your request as pulling rank," she added, trying to lighten the intensity of their conversation.

"Do you like Chinese food?"

"Sure," she blurted out, immediately regretting it. Michael Jordan spelled trouble, and she was diving headfirst into the deep end.

"I'll pick you up at seven."

AT SIX-THIRTY, Ashley stood in front of the armoire, scowling at her wardrobe. When he'd walked her to her newly replaced rental car, Michael advised her to dress casually. When she traveled out of town on a job, she packed suits and dresses that disguised her free-spirited side. Those who only knew her as a no-nonsense businesswoman would be shocked to see her dressed in oversize sweaters, and gauzy, long skirts she loved to hunt down in vintage clothing stores. Ashley recognized that tailored suits were an integral part of her professional identity. That identity was very important to her, so she didn't mind the sacrifice.

She had brought a few casual outfits for the times she'd be able to sneak away and do what she wanted. There was no way she would let Michael see her dressed in those. She needed to present herself as unobtainable. She wasn't certain how he'd maneuvered her into spending the evening with him. As a rule she was assertive enough to stonewall anyone continuing to coerce her after she had given an adamant no. With Michael, she'd caved in after only a couple of ineffectual protests. Besides, if she didn't hurry, he would be at the door while she was still dithering around, dressed only in a dove-gray chemise.

Ashley finally pulled on a charcoal linen dirndl skirt and muted print blouse. Her sole concession to casualness would be not to wear her suit jacket. She made a moue at the vanity mirror. No doubt about it, her mouth was too wide and, worse, her bottom lip looked pouty. She wore pale gloss rather than lipstick, to downplay her full lips.

Checking her watch, she cursed. She'd taken down her chignon to relieve a headache and now there wasn't time to get it back up. "Which is worse?" she muttered. "Meeting Michael with curling hair or letting him pick me up at the door, as if we're going on a date?" No contest. Intent on getting to the lobby fast, she hurried into the suite's living room. That afternoon the airline had delivered her suitcase containing her raincoat and umbrella and she grabbed them on the run.

A loud knock shook the French door that opened onto an eight-story atrium. Through the gathered casement drapes, she saw Michael leaning against the frame, one hand inserted in his jacket pocket. She opened the door and they gave each other a nerve-tingling once-over.

Oh, deliver me! He's a jock! Michael wore dark blue pants with a white stripe down each side, a red knit polo shirt that had a yellow-and-blue collar, and a khaki jacket, its sleeves pushed back on his forearms. Weren't jocks supposed to be ugly and consequently easy to dismiss?

"You call this casual?" He saw her objection forming and quickly added, "Never mind, you look great. Forget I said anything." He stepped inside without an invitation. "Not bad for a hotel." Striding over to the small pullman kitchen, he checked out its compact refrigerator and oven. "You can even cook here if you want."

"A real bonus," Ashley mumbled under her breath as she trailed him down the short hall. He peeked into the bathroom and continued on to the bedroom. "I think this is where I demand to see your search warrant."

"Don't mind me. I'm the curious sort." He opened both of the twin armoires, one concealing a television, the other her clothes.

She stepped forward, ready to intervene in case he decided to investigate her lingerie drawer. That would be an ironclad case of invasion of privacy.

Her fingers tightened on the umbrella when he tested the king-size bed with one knee. Maybe he was only curious; nevertheless, his closeness and the implied intimacy of his actions made her hold her breath. "If we're going to meet that plane, don't you think we should be on our way?"

"Hmm? Oh, sure. I'm ready when you are."

Ashley gulped, knowing she ought to have begged off with a headache. The excuse was commonplace and boring, but less provocative and safer than the sensations and scenarios evoked by observing Michael resting his leg on her bed.

"It's stopped raining," he said, indicating the coat draped over her arm. "Why didn't you wear that this morning when you needed it?"

Relieved that he didn't seem to be suffering from the same X-rated fantasy as she, Ashley led him down the hallway. "It's a long story, but basically I came here and my suitcase went to Denver."

"Another statistic to add to those lost-baggage figures they publish every month, huh?"

She busied herself locking the door and getting to the elevator, purposely neglecting to mention that the snafu was her fault. Running late, she'd given the harried curbside handler an old itinerary and he'd tagged her suitcase for Colorado. Such confusion and mix-ups, unfortunately, were a fact of life for her.

She looked around for Michael's Agnes, remembering her overflowing back seat. Should she offer to drive her rental? She suppressed that suggestion when Michael escorted her to another car. Ashley ran a finger along the shiny, rounded, turquoise fender of a mid-fifties Buick Roadmaster and laughed with delight. Michael joined in, obviously pleased.

"I figured you'd be impressed. It's a hand-me-down from my grandmother," he explained.

"Of course, I'm impressed. I don't know anyone else who has an ICK," she said, pointing to the three chrome letters on the side.

"The *B* and the *U* got lost a couple of years back. I'm still scouring salvage yards for replacements."

"It's in great condition otherwise."

"Grandma babied this car for twenty-two years. I've tried to treat it just as gently." He opened the door and handed her inside. She was still smiling when he slid into the opposite seat. "Care to let me in on the joke?"

"This morning when you made that crack about the kind of car I drive, I almost laughed. Mine is a fifties car, too."

"No kidding? A Buick?"

"No, an MG."

"An old Morris Garage. That's a real classic. What model?" They accelerated onto the freeway that ran in front of her hotel.

"It's a TD that Aunt Kitty gave me for high-school graduation. She found it on a trip to England and had it shipped over for me."

"That's some nice aunt you have. Those eyes and a vintage MG, too. What did she give your sister? Blue-chip stocks?"

How odd that he remembered those brief references to her relatives. She'd have to be more careful about letting personal revelations slip. "Cooper got a trunkful of heirloom sterling. Ten-piece place settings, service for twenty-four. She was truly ecstatic. I tell you, it's a moving experience to watch someone become rapturous over silverware."

"It's probably appreciated more than your car," he said, changing lanes. "In value, I mean."

"Maybe. But my aunt is a good judge of what suits each of us the best." Cooper had been groomed from the cradle to plan sit-down dinners for two dozen people—a patently useless talent in Ashley's book. She'd rather zip around in her MG.

"How do you keep the thing running? Those cars need a lot of tinkering, and at the risk of sounding chauvinistic, I can't see you spending much time under a hood."

"I wouldn't know a point from a piston," she agreed, unoffended. "But I have an arrangement with the owner of a foreign-car repair shop. I keep his books, do all his government reports and file his tax returns. In exchange, George makes sure the MG is ready when I want to drive it. It works well for both of us."

Michael negotiated the interchange from one freeway onto another. The heavy car seemed to glide just above the road surface, immune to cracks and potholes.

"Where are we going?" She had assumed they would eat somewhere along the Bloomington Strip, the area near her hotel that was lined with restaurants.

"Downtown."

"You go downtown at night? To eat?"

"Sure. We go downtown for everything. The stadium, movies, Guthrie Theater, Walker Art Center, Orchestra Hall, the best shopping."

"I haven't been to downtown Atlanta in over a year."

"Then you're in for a treat."

Within minutes Michael had eased the old Buick into a parallel space and they'd walked the half block to Nicollet Mall, which was open only to pedestrian and bus traffic. The street was the hub of city-center activity. In spite of her traumatic first day, Ashley had already decided she liked Minneapolis. After three years of steady travel, she'd developed an instinct for knowing right away which places appealed to her.

There was something irresistible about a city that planted trees and flowers on its main street, then piped classical music through speakers for a concert-in-the-park atmosphere. Michael told her to wait until winter, when the sidewalk was defrosted by underground heaters.

She had a momentary vision—impossible and eerie—of herself strolling down Nicollet wearing boots and a heavy coat, accompanied by the sound of Christmas carols. "The longest an audit's ever taken was eight weeks. Since it's April, I don't think there's any danger I'll be here when it snows."

"Stranger things have happened," he said, eyeing a pair of leather-jacketed teenage boys who overtook them, then turned around to check Ashley out.

She laughed when one of them sent her a sly wink before cockily sauntering on his way. "If we have to stay here that long, Mr. Jordan, I guarantee you're gonna be in a heap o' trouble."

He said something under his breath she couldn't catch. She watched a small, stoop-shouldered lady struggling to pull along a shopping car loaded with packages. Twice she had to stop and redistribute the weight. Ashley grew alarmed at the sight of the two boys separating and siding up on the tiny, defenseless woman.

She dashed over toward her, calling over her shoulder to Michael. "They're going to mug her!"

"Ashley, wait a minute! Come back here."

"Hurry! We've got to help!" She sprinted ahead without waiting for him. Her low-heeled shoes made running easy, but Michael caught up to her within seconds.

"Ashley, I think you jumped the gun," he said dryly, lightly grasping her arm to halt her.

"What's wrong with you? Can't you see she's in danger?"

"You'd better take a second look," he advised with amusement.

"What do you mean?" Ashley asked, but she had a sinking sensation that her impetuous side had taken over yet again. She gazed ahead to where the two boys had lifted the uncooperative cart, carrying it between them. Their alleged "victim" was talking animatedly and patting both their backs in gratitude.

It was too much to bear on the first day of a new assignment, when establishing her professionalism was so essential. That damned alarm clock! Everything had started to go wrong the moment she'd let it wake her up that morning. Now there was probably no way she could redeem herself.

Michael guided her up Sixth Street, grumbling good-naturedly that he'd better check that his insurance premiums were paid up-to-date since hanging around her was bound to involve him in one confrontation after another.

Ashley felt like explaining that the whole day had been a terrible mistake; that she'd got up on the wrong foot. She really needed to correct the impression she had given him so far. Otherwise he might conclude she was another flighty female who had no place meddling in men's business.

She had struggled so hard not to be compared with women like her mother and sister. The possibility Michael might see her that way was enough to bring on an anxiety attack.

"You're probably wondering how a person who gets herself into as much trouble as I have today can head the review team of a reliable audit." She had to assure him of her competence. Even wizards like Michael Jordan suffered downtimes. "Surely you've had days when nothing goes right from the minute you wake up."

She took his murmur as agreement and pressed on. "It doesn't happen to me often, but this has been one for the record." He gave her a noncommittal nod, which didn't offer her much reassurance.

Inside the mall, they entered the Chinese restaurant and were led up a wide staircase to the second level of an immense Oriental dining room. As soon as they were seated and given menus, Michael recommended the beef rice and chicken and wonton with Chinese vegetables.

"Could you please give us separate checks?" she requested of the departing waiter.

Michael shook his head. "You're determined to provoke me about this, aren't you?"

Ashley flushed, stating her reasons calmly. "There's no reason for you to buy my dinner. I'm on an expense account. The company expects me to pay for my meals."

"To hell with the company!" He slouched against his chair back and took a deep breath. "Ashley, get it through your obstinate head. The only reason I asked you out is that I want to be with you." Leaning toward her, his voice was part growl, part whisper. "Honey, this is a date. Remember that. And if you're real lucky, I won't make a pass when I take you back to the hotel."

Her heart had done a funny little skip at his use of "honey." No one ever called her that. She wouldn't tolerate it. She simply couldn't allow him to affect her that way. "Bear in mind I may have been lying when I disclaimed knowledge of karate."

"Consider me forewarned," he said, flashing her a smile. "Now, since we've already met, let's get on with the preliminaries."

She was clearly not sitting across from the prototypical company vice president. This man was on the prowl, and Ashley was ill-equipped to deal with him. She had better send him a message that she was uninterested and unavailable. "Tell me, do you put the make on all visiting auditors?"

He didn't even blink. "I don't put the make on anybody. Until today, I've gone out of my way to avoid visiting auditors. That's what delegation is for. I know you people are a necessary evil but everyone starts scrambling for vacation time when they hear you're on the way.

"You, however," he went on, "are a different matter, and subtlety isn't my long suit. I say what's on my mind. I like other people to do the same. Dancing with your intentions complicates things. I hate complications." He spooned hot mustard and sweet-and-sour sauce onto the spring roll that had just been served.

Ashley concentrated on her own egg roll while racking her brain for a clever comeback. What she wanted to say, and what she ought to, were at war inside her head.

"No comment?"

She chewed slowly, aware that his blunt honesty demanded the same from her. "I don't run across straightforward people very often. I haven't had much practice in handling them." Nor did she possess the ability to cope with a male in pursuit. It was not a skill she'd ever expected to need.

"Then maybe you've been spending time with the wrong people."

Implying, she presumed, he was the right sort of person to spend time with. She looked for a hint of levity, but his expression was serious. If she had a lick of sense, she'd invent some excuse and get away from him now. Instead, she refilled their teacups and faced him with a brave smile. "What sort of preliminaries are you interested in?"

"You know. The usual kind of banter people engage in when they're trying to take each other's measure."

"Sounds suspiciously like the 'dancing' you say you detest."

He lifted one shoulder. "A certain amount is unavoidable at the beginning. Let's hurry and get it out of the way so we can go on to the good stuff." He drained the tea from his small cup. "Let's see, I know you're from Charleston. Where did you go when you left there?"

"To Michigan State for four years, then graduate school at the University of Texas. After that, I took a job with a Big Eight, moved to Atlanta, and stayed with them long enough to pass my CPA exam. Now I'm on the road for our company." She could see Michael doing some fast calculations.

"A well-planned career, Ms. Atwood. The right schools, advanced degree, excellent work experience. I'd say you've been on a straight path all the way. An enviable record for someone who's twenty-eight?"

Ashley nodded. From his tone, she had a strong inkling he hadn't finished with the subject.

"I'll bet you intend to break off sometime soon, start your own firm. Right?"

"Maybe. If I ever decide where I want to live permanently." Naturally, such a move would indicate that she'd chosen to live a more traditional life—a prospect that filled Ashley with inexplicable panic. Traveling was easier.

"A fast-tracker." He made it sound like a disease more gruesome than bubonic plague or leprosy. "Hell-bent on succeeding in business, no matter what else suffers."

Why should he be so caustic about her career goals? "I don't think of myself that way. I'm good at my work, so I've channeled most of my time and energy into it, like lots of people do. If you don't take your job seriously when you're trying to get established, you'll be sorry later."

"If you say so," Michael assented with a decided lack of enthusiasm. "There are so many other things to do apart from work—more interesting, more fun things. What do you do for fun, Ashley, when you have time off in Atlanta?"

"First thing, I sleep for about twenty-four hours straight. Then I catch up with friends, go to antique shows, flea markets or estate and garage sales looking for hatpins to add to my collection." To a jock, those sedentary pastimes must sound pretty tame. What she enjoyed most about her hobby was the eccentrics she befriended. That was the real reason she kept collecting.

She could have told him about haunting cemeteries all over the country—the older the better—in search of humorous epitaphs for the book she intended to compile one day. That would only reinforce her own eccentricity.

He grinned. "Hatpins, huh? Well, everybody needs a hobby, I suppose."

"Yes. Imagining yours makes me tired." She felt color mottle her cheeks, realizing how he might interpret her words. "Your clothes, I mean," she said, pointing to his sporty outfit. "You look like someone who thrives on getting physical." *Keep it up, Ashley. Maybe you can say something really embarrassing if you try hard enough.*

His half smile said he knew exactly what she meant, but that this time, he'd let her off the hook.

Their entrees arrived, providing her with a diversion from the corner she'd talked herself into. Ashley's eyes widened at the huge bowl of chicken and wontons surrounded by Chinese vegetables.

Michael laughed. "I hope you're hungry. Of course, I can be bribed into helping you out."

Digging in, they talked and ate until, unbelievably, every bite disappeared. Yet it seemed only minutes had passed when he signaled the waiter. "We've got about half an hour to get to the airport. That should put us there right on time." He asked their waiter for the check and steered her out the door. Before she had a chance to protest, they were back on the freeway. Michael had an insidious way of getting what he wanted in spite of her best efforts to stay in charge.

The plane landed on time, and Jack Thompson and Mark Gordon were among the first passengers off. Both men were tall, at least six-two. Mark had a slim elegance accentuated by the European tailoring of his suits, and his graceful movements were suave and urbane. On the other hand, Jack was about as polished as a Mack truck. His broad shoulders and thick neck attested to his years of college football. It was too bad he tried to emulate Mark. He didn't stand a chance.

Mark spotted Ashley and waved. Such a display would have spoiled Jack's tenuous hold on cool, so he saved his greeting until they were face-to-face. "Hello, boss. The slaves are here. Where's your whip?"

Ashley smiled at the barb. Jack never failed to slip in a sardonic reference to her position as senior member of the audit team. Once he finished his macho posturing, they got along well enough.

"Hi, Jack. How's tricks?"

Jack made no secret of his fondness for adding names to his little black book. Usually Ashley refused to let him goad her into commenting on his extracurricular activities. For a few seconds, he looked abashed that she'd mentioned it now. Soon enough, he recovered his aplomb.

"What can I say? If you've got it . . ." His words trailed off suggestively. Thankfully they were spared his old standard, "Use it or lose it."

Mark entered the conversation. "Hello, honey girl. It's been a long time."

He used the nickname that a Yankee acquaintance had pinned on her because of her background and accent. Mark was the only company employee whom Ashley saw socially. They shared the same group of friends in Atlanta. "For a while, it looked as if we were never going to hit the same town at the same time. It's good to see you at last."

Mark's attention shifted to Michael, and Ashley sensed a sudden wariness in both men. It was subdued but definitely there. She made the introductions, noting Jack's and Mark's surprise when she added Michael's title. They were astonished to be chauffeured by the head honcho. The minute they had her alone, they'd demand to know why. She could satisfy Jack with any plausible explanation; Mark, however, would be suspicious—for a man, he was amazingly perceptive.

On the drive back, Jack pumped Michael about nightlife in the Twin Cities. *The list is certainly endless,* Ashley thought, peeved at Michael's ability to reel off one hot spot after another. Her mouth drew into a tight line as she imagined him hanging out in clubs, picking up women, drinking and carousing until all hours. Of course, it was *no* business of hers.

"Come on, Miss Priss," Jack chided. "Don't begrudge me a little fun because you're such a stick-in-the-mud."

Ashley stifled a grin. She'd done a phenomenal job disguising the more eccentric aspects of her personality. Mark could furnish plenty of incidents demonstrating how scatterbrained she could be. But he was a good friend, and extremely discreet.

When they arrived at the hotel, Jack and Mark stopped at the registration desk. Michael continued on to the elevators.

"You don't have to go with me," Ashley interjected. "I'm able to ride up on my own."

He hit the call button and gave her a now familiar look of frustration. "You're beginning to sound like a broken record on what you don't need me to do." He tugged her inside while he talked. "I know all about liberated women. My mother has indoctrinated the whole family on that issue." His smile was more ironic than amused. "She also taught me to always see a lady to her door. She'd skin me if I forgot my manners." He punched seven.

Sensing the futility of protest, Ashley watched through the glass sides as the plant-filled courtyard receded beneath them, almost convincing herself that the elevator's movement was causing the fluttering feeling in her stomach.

"Ash," Michael said solemnly, "I don't go to any of those places I told Jack about. That's not my style."

Great glory! He reads minds! "You don't owe me an explanation. Why should I care whether you go to clubs or not?" she replied.

"I guess you can answer that better than I."

She silently averted her eyes.

When they reached her door, he took the key and unlocked it, making no move to come inside. She was relieved until he asked, "Is there something between you and Mark that I need to worry about?"

"What do you mean, 'something between us'? Why would you worry?"

"Ashley, don't be coy. Just tell me, are you two friends . . . casual dates . . . lovers?"

She chuckled at the last idea. No one who knew her well would even have hinted at such a relationship. Although it would be safer and easier to let him think she was involved with Mark, she couldn't willfully mislead anyone. "Mark's a terrific person, a good friend. He is also carrying a torch the size of Texas for an adventurous redhead who struck out to mine opals in Australia."

"Good." Michael cleared his throat and took a step closer. "That makes things simpler."

Resting both hands lightly on her shoulders, he looked into her eyes. His lips parted and Ashley's breath caught at the promise of their soft, inviting touch. Instead, his hands moved up slowly to frame her face. One thumb whisked over her lower lip, back and forth in a hypnotically seductive motion that held her captive as securely as chains.

Finally he spoke, his voice a low rasp. "Night, Ashley Atwood. Sweet dreams."

He might as well have kissed her. The effect was fully as potent.

3

"SWEET DREAMS, INDEED," Ashley scoffed as she brewed herself a cup of strong tea at the courtyard breakfast buffet. Michael Jordan had put a curse on her with his parting words last night. *Sweet* described pleasant, soothing visions that left you relaxed and rested. Her "sweet" dreams had been provocative and disturbing. For someone who'd refined sleeping to a fine art, she resented being repeatedly awakened by a restless, almost feverish yearning she refused to succumb to.

"Must have been some party," Jack observed when Ashley settled into a chair beneath the striped-umbrellaed table. "You look like the devil."

So much for the restorative powers of makeup. A general application of foundation evidently hadn't concealed the circles under her eyes. "Such flattery, Jack. It's easy to see why you're a hit with the opposite sex."

"Looks like you're not doing so bad in that department yourself. Talk about a fast mover." He looked to Mark for agreement, but Mark was watching Ashley. "In town one day, and already you've snared a vice president."

"Don't be asinine! I haven't *snared* anyone. Nor am I likely to. If I look wiped out, it's because yesterday was very trying." She related the story of her accident, claiming that aches and bruises had kept her awake. It was a bald-faced lie. Luckily Jack didn't catch on.

Mark, however, wasn't so gullible. He knew it would take more than a minor shake-up to deprive Ashley of sleep. "Have you run into problems with the audit?"

"Oho, that's a laugh," Jack said around a mouthful of scrambled eggs. "Everyone knows an audit is never a problem for our Killer Mole."

Despite her preoccupation, Ashley had to smile. She knew that within company circles she'd earned the nickname Killer Mole because of her talent for digging up even the most minor deviations from prescribed company procedures. It wasn't the primary purpose of her job and she didn't care to foster the reputation; it was just that when she got involved with numbers and their accompanying paper trail, discrepancies leaped out at her, begging to be reported.

Riding down to meet her co-workers, she'd reminded herself of those responsibilities. She had to forget all that had happened the day before. The parking-lot episode and her fantasies about Michael were missteps. She was determined to start fresh today, and to treat this audit the same as any other. Mr. Michael Jordan would be consigned to the background.

By noon, Ashley realized she'd been overly optimistic. Forcing herself to focus and concentrate, she was able to make up some of yesterday's lost time. Still, Michael's invitation to lunch—even though he included Jack and Mark—was more than she could face.

Using personal business as her excuse for not going out, she watched the three men leave, then took the fire stairs to the basement. She remembered there was a cot in an inner room of the ladies' lounge, and resting there interested her more than food. After ten minutes of willing her eyes to stay closed, all hope of sleep vanished when she heard two women talking on the other side of the closed door.

"Wonder why Michael's lady auditor didn't go to lunch with him today. I know he asked. I couldn't believe my eyes when I saw them eating together yesterday. A first!"

Ashley struggled to sit up. She prayed that the two would remain where they were, because there was no place to hide.

The second woman added, "Speaking of eyes, have you noticed how he watches her, especially if he thinks no one else is looking? What I can't figure out is why he picked someone so uptight. That man needs a *woman*, if you catch my drift." The voice lowered, turned sultry. "You bet if he looked at me that way, just once, I'd give him anything he wanted, no questions asked."

Her friend laughed. "Don't hold your breath. Something tells me you're not his type."

"Who knows what his type is? Have you ever seen him with anybody? Ever heard him mention a special woman outside of work? He always comes alone to the two company parties every year. Talk about carrying the term 'private life' to extremes! It hurts to think of all that delicious masculinity going to waste. Give me one night with him and I'd show—"

"Down, girl," her companion cautioned. "I worked for a company once where the guy in charge considered every female employee fair game. I'll take Michael's professionalism and detachment any day. It's a heck of a lot easier to find someone to keep you warm at night than it is to find a good boss."

"You might be right. But I still wouldn't mind trading shoes with Ms. Atwood. I'll bet when he turns on the heat he can really..."

The voices faded, and Ashley leaped to her feet. The small room was closing in on her. She couldn't rush out, for fear of encountering the two women who'd discussed Michael. She dampened a paper towel with cold water and bathed her heated face while she reran their conversation. Never had she been fodder for the rumor mill on a job. She had no idea how to combat it.

When she couldn't stand being trapped for another second, she fled. Claudia found her frantically feeding coins to a vending machine, accumulating a pile of cellophane-wrapped snack packages.

"Ashley, are you all right? You look kind of feverish."

"Just hot and thirsty," she croaked. Ashley popped the top on an orange soda and took a series of slurpy swallows.

"Better?" Claudia asked when Ashley stopped drinking long enough to make a face at the can.

"No. I hate orange soda." Claudia refrained from pointing out the obvious. "And I hate being gossiped about."

"Uh-oh. The office grapevine must have kicked into high gear. To be expected, I guess, after the boss asked you to lunch two days in a row." Claudia expressed her opinion with a dismissing flick of one hand. "You know how it is in places like this. Everyone wants to know everyone else's business. And Michael is a prime topic for speculation, mainly because he never gives them anything really juicy to chew on. His love life is this company's best-kept secret."

"Love life! What's that got to do with me?"

Claudia shrugged. "Nothing—or lots. Trust me, I'm no more privy to what Michael does after hours than the rest. The difference is, I don't want to be. I have a gorgeous hunk of a husband who takes care of all my interests in that area."

"But I don't—I can't—What I'm trying to say is that it's important to maintain high standards, not leave myself open to accusations of unprofessionalism."

"Aw, lighten up," Claudia advised. "You're taking this too seriously and too personally. People are gonna talk, no matter what. That's how most of them relieve the tedium of work. Let them have their entertainment. I'm sure it won't damage your credibility in any way."

Ashley wished she felt comforted by Claudia's reassurances. She hastened back to work with a purseful of junk food and a foreboding that the gossip had only begun.

For the remainder of the week, no matter how often Ashley berated herself, she nurtured a guilty pleasure in her anticipation that Michael would ask her out again. Naturally, it was a foregone conclusion she'd have to decline. The chance never came.

Perhaps he'd decided it was occupational suicide to become involved with someone who worked for the same company. Indeed, she had told him as much. He hadn't paid attention at first. Sometime between then and now, he had lost interest. Why should that surprise her? She recognized she lacked the mysterious quality that attracted a man to a woman. Still, it was humbling to realize she'd misjudged his reasons for dropping by the conference room so often. She had apparently misinterpreted all those times his eyes made contact and held for a few seconds longer than necessary. Naively she assumed the heightened awareness was mutual.

To take her mind off the whole dismal matter, she spent Saturday playing tourist in St. Paul with Jack and Mark. As a remedy, sight-seeing had only limited success. When the two men announced plans to have brunch downtown the next day and take in a Twins game, Ashley was almost desperate enough to go along. Never mind that she loathed baseball.

Instead she chose to go solo and planned to visit the city's oldest cemetery. Finding out she could reserve a red convertible had lifted her spirits right away, and she hurried to get dressed so she could claim it.

There was just one minor glitch: she found herself locked in her room.

Forty-five minutes later, she was still locked inside. At least the hotel personnel weren't treating her as if she were drunk or demented. "Making any progress?" she called to the maintenance man who'd had to be summoned from home.

"Some," he replied laconically, attacking the mechanism with yet another gadget. "Try to stay calm."

Ashley bit back the urge for a few seconds, then gave in to it and yelled, "I *am* calm! Just get this damned thing open!" With the way her luck was running, of course, that was the moment Michael picked to show up at her door. "I swear you must have radar that signals you every time my dignity deserts me."

He grinned at her through the glass. Then he picked up another tool and offered it to the maintenance man. It turned out to be the right one, and the door swung open.

"I've heard of people being locked out, Ash," Michael said, stepping inside. "It takes a real knack to get locked in. How did you manage that?"

"Don't push it," she warned. "My temper is a little uneven at this point." She snatched a fringed denim jacket from the couch, knowing that holding it in front of her was like closing the henhouse after the fox's visit. Michael had already seen the fluorescent-yellow bike pants and purple shirt—the very antithesis of her accountant's habit.

"Nice outfit. I especially like the socks." They were purple, to match her sneakers, with tiny bananas on the cuffs that clicked when she walked. "Going someplace special?"

"Uh, not exactly," she fibbed, trying to cook up a plausible explanation for her appearance. "Just . . . out."

"Good. If you're not headed anywhere special, you're free to go with me. I have something to show you in Winona, so let's hit the road."

Since he'd had a rebuttal for every argument, Ashley had given in, and allowed herself to be hustled into Agnes. They were traveling south along the Mississippi River.

"This reminds me of the kidnapping plot-device in historical romances," she mused, "where the pirate hero spirits the heroine onto his ship and—"

"Ravishes her before journey's end," he finished, wicked intent lighting his eyes.

"How do you know about such things?" She shouldn't have confessed to reading those books. Like the clothes, a taste for romance novels didn't fit an accountant's profile.

"Last summer, when my brother and I teased our sister about toting a shopping bag full of them up to the lake, she set us straight. Informed us that if men were even half interested in what women want, in fulfilling their fantasies, they'd read every romance novel ever published."

Ashley raised both brows. "I can imagine how you and your brother received that suggestion."

"Never let it be said that Doug and I aren't willing to benefit from a little sisterly advice. Each of us read some of them, then compared notes."

"And?"

"My lips are sealed. Women do not like men who kiss and tell."

"They also do not like men who are full of—"

His laugh drowned out her final word, which was a blessing. She'd blundered badly enough by coming along with him. No need to compound the folly. Still, she couldn't sit silent and stiff as a stump, so Ashley confined her comments to work and compliments on the beauty of the foliage lining the highway.

They eventually arrived at Winona, then bounced down a road that ran parallel to the river. Michael pulled up to the end of a landing dock before halting Agnes.

"Oh, it's wonderful!" Ashley exclaimed, forgetting her vow to act reserved in spite of her outfit. In front of them was a houseboat mounted atop fifty-five-gallon drums and tethered fore and aft with heavy cables. Its deck and cabin had aged without benefit of paint.

"My version of a pirate ship," Michael explained, following her onto the gangway.

Battling visions of being ravished, she asked, "Is this where you live?"

"No. I use it as a retreat." He unlocked the door and gestured for her to precede him inside.

The one-room interior was neat, designed to make the most of limited space. The upriver end had floor-to-ceiling shelves crammed with books, a cassette player, speakers and tapes. The opposite end contained a corner head, a tiny galley and fold-out tables and benches. Along the water side was a built-in single bunk with drawers below it.

Michael leaned over to raise the woven shade on a large window above his bed and cranked open the glass jalousie slats to let in fresh air. "What do you think?"

"I . . . It's very cozy. It's a perfect getaway spot." What looked even more perfect was the play of muscles under his plaid shirt. Her gaze strayed downward. His faded jeans, clung snugly to his tush like a lover's hands. Ashley swallowed and raised her sightline to the outside view. "Do you spend a lot of time here?"

"Depends. If I'm in the mood to paint, I may come every weekend. Then again, I might not get down for several months. I like the quiet and isolation."

Again Ashley was struck by the contradictions in him. People who based their success on balanced columns of figures and bottom lines generally approached life pragmatically rather than creatively.

Michael's artistic bent was one more intriguing element. One more temptation she didn't need.

She wandered over to an enlarged photograph of a boulder-rimmed waterfall hanging next to an oil painting of the same scene. The initials MPJ were in the lower right corner. "You did this?"

"I did. As you can see, my technique leaves a lot to be desired." He crossed the cabin to gaze at his canvas. "I'm strictly an amateur. No training at all. Painting pleases me, so I keep at it." He tapped the framed photo. "Though I'm better with a camera than a brush, I don't enjoy it as much."

To her, he appeared to have plenty of talent. She moved to another photo farther down the wall. "This is your family?"

"Yep. All the Jordans. Taken a while back when everyone went up to the lake house. We were celebrating my mom's college graduation, thirty years later than she originally planned."

Ashley recalled the Atwood family portrait hanging in their parlor, every member formally posed and smiling. In contrast, Michael's family were leaning against one another and laughing.

"You all look so happy," she said softly, unable to mask the wistfulness she felt.

Michael's hand rested gently on her shoulder. "Until recently my family has stayed close. We actually like each other, which makes us the exception, I think.

Most people's relatives give them more headaches than happiness." He turned her to face him. "Is that how it is for you?"

He had a way of hitting the essentials. "The Atwoods are difficult to describe. Let's say that I don't fit their mold," she replied, unable to disguise her resentment.

Her shoulder muscles tightened beneath his hand as he guided her toward the bunk and urged her to sit on one end while he took the opposite.

"My parents met and married within a month," he told her. "They're still together after thirty-five years." For a few seconds Michael stared out the window. "There have been some ups and downs, especially lately. Hopefully, they can weather the storm. You don't just throw away something like that if you're lucky enough to find it in the first place."

Hearing the emotion in his voice, Ashley looked into his eyes. "You're right. I don't think either of my parents has ever regretted their match. They love each other as much as ever. That's not the same as what your mother and father share. I could tell just by looking at the picture. You're fortunate to have been a part of that."

"For years, Mom and Dad really talked up the idea of all of us getting married. Guess they wanted their children to have what they've had. So far it's eluded us all. I'm thirty-four, Doug is thirty-two and Diana's thirty. Before they were our ages, they already had three kids. Here we are—not one of us has found the perfect soulmate."

Ashley's heart hammered erratically. How did he do this to her? He'd made a simple statement on the marital status of himself and his siblings. It had nothing to do with her. Yet, for a second, he'd looked at her as if she were his soul mate. No, she'd only imagined it.

She got up and walked back over to the photo for a closer look. The family resemblance was unmistakable; even his parents looked somewhat alike. Like Michael, the rest of the Jordans were tall and slender, with brown hair and eyes. "Do they live near you?"

"Only Doug. He's with an airline based in Minneapolis so we see a lot of each other. My parents live in D.C. and Diana teaches at the American school in Brussels. She likes to travel in Europe and doesn't come back to the States too often. We haven't gotten together much the past couple of years. Mom's been so immersed in starting her business, and she used to be the one insisting on regular reunions."

"I see," Ashley murmured, absorbed in the picture, aware of the eerie pull it created upon her. Then she blurted out something she'd never revealed to anyone. "When I was a child, I was positive gypsies had left me on the Atwood doorstep by mistake. How else could I explain being so unlike them?"

"And now?" he asked.

"I'm still unsure." Her laugh was strained.

He kneaded her shoulders, then let his hands slide slowly down her arms to grasp both hands, giving them a gentle squeeze. Ashley wasn't used to needing comfort. For a brief time Michael offered it and she accepted it. The moment passed and she moved away. Closeness was too risky. She shouldn't even be here. Michael made her wish they'd met under different circumstances; that she could have a different destiny.

Michael hadn't anticipated bringing Ashley here would depress her. Somehow it had. After five days of telling himself that his first impression of her had been wrong, and that she was just another tight-assed accountant, he couldn't quite accept it. He felt compelled to try again. When he'd seen those outrageous clothes, and her ponytail swinging, he knew his instincts had been right. He'd found the parking-lot demon again. All this family talk had depressed her and he needed to change the mood. Reaching for the door, he suggested, "Why don't you dig out a blanket from under that bunk? We can spread it on the deck and eat our picnic in the sun." He tapped his watch. "Can't have you turning into a grouch because I haven't fed you lunch."

"Food?" She smiled and went to fetch the blanket. "Mr. Jordan, you're a man after my heart."

Michael smiled as he strode over to the gangplank. He wasn't quite ready to factor hearts into the equation—not that he had anything against getting serious with the right woman. But before reaching that point, he needed to discover the real Ashley.

He crossed the deck and watched her soaking up the sun's rays, her eyes closed. Braced on her forearms, she was semireclined on a colorful quilt. The crisscrossed front of her shirt gaped open, revealing the hot-pink tube that clung to her breasts, outlining her nipples. He felt like an adolescent again, when a furtive peek at a girl's bra strap was paradise.

Give me strength! Michael sat down, placing a wicker basket between them, before what he was feeling became obvious to Ashley. Ashley stirred to peek inside.

"I'm impressed. Now, this is a picnic!" She eyed the artfully arranged tray. "Looks yummy."

"I'll take credit for the idea, but Byerly's did the rest." He uncorked a thermos of lemonade. "I can put on a good spread myself, though."

"Since I'm a complete disaster in the kitchen, I'll be easy to convince." She sipped some lemonade and grinned at him.

He chuckled. "I love to eat, so I decided long ago that I'd have to learn to cook. Mom made all of us take turns fixing meals so we'd know the basics."

"Smart lady," she said, wondering how it would have been to grow up with a mother like that. Her own had been more concerned with knowing the right people, belonging to the right organizations and bemoaning her fate because Ashley didn't act like a lady. The closest Eleanor Atwood came to household chores was making sure the servants had done them. Ashley abhorred the relationships between the Atwood family and their "staff." She'd left all that behind.

"Open," Michael requested, teasing her lips with something cold and tangy.

She tugged a marinated shrimp from the wooden pick. When his teeth immediately sank into the next one on the skewer, she stopped chewing. There was something unbearably intimate about his mouth closing over where hers had been only seconds before. She touched her lips, surprised to feel them warm, tingly, almost as if they'd been kissed—long and hard and expertly.

In turmoil, Ashley stared into the water's green depths. For nearly a week she'd been guarding against Michael's sensual magnetism, trying to resist it. After he had backed off for several days, she assumed she could be with him without succumbing to the attraction. Instead, it was stronger than ever.

"I don't remember the last time I went on a picnic," she remarked, seeking some means to stifle her longings.

He popped a cherry tomato stuffed with crabmeat into her mouth. "See what you city girls miss."

She savored the treat, watching him devour another shrimp. "Don't say that with so much disapproval. You live in the city, too."

"Only so I can afford this—" he rapped the boat's planked deck "—and my hobbies, traveling. My career will never be my life and it won't define my identity. I enjoy it just as I do lots of other things. But if I were independently wealthy, I might not bother with a regular job." When she didn't respond, he shrugged. "Now I suppose you think I'm hopeless, lazy and lacking in ambition."

"Of course not," Ashley replied. He couldn't be, to get as far as he had. It was his other dimensions, however, which appealed to her. "It's just that most people I know are pretty single-minded about being professionally successful. So am I."

This time she received a white asparagus spear in a tissue-thin wrapping of ham. "You've never had the urge to chuck it all and sail to Tahiti or surf the world's great waves?"

Ashley giggled, as if the idea of herself doing either was preposterous. Actually, it was enormously enticing, especially the Tahiti part. But she wouldn't confess to it. "I know that the day we met, I must have come off as the ditz queen of the universe. Most of the time I fit everyone's stereotype of a plodding accountant." She doggedly continued, although she sensed he wasn't buying her self-description. "Those outbursts were an aberration, believe me."

"Here, try this." He rewarded her with a cream-dipped strawberry. "Why is it so important to convince me how dull and traditional you are? Spontaneity isn't a crime, Ash."

Not as long as she wasn't the one being spontaneous. "You're the only person who's ever called me Ash."

"You mind?"

"I guess not." *Except it's one more thing that sets you apart from everyone else.* "My sister used to try to bait me by calling me Ashtray." Her eyes danced with remembered mischief. "Which forced me to retaliate with Chicken Coop. Unimaginative, but effective."

She accepted a second strawberry. The Devonshire cream tasted luscious, and Ashley stared hungrily at the trace of it left on Michael's lower lip, wishing she could sample that. She shook her head slightly and started to speak. The words backed up in her throat.

He bit the tip off a huge berry, then extended the remainder to her. Her eyes locked with his, she took a bite. Juice welled up over her lips and trickled onto his fingers. She felt a tremor in Michael's hand; his eyes turned dark and avid. She'd never been the object of such explicit masculine desire, but there was no mistaking the power of it.

She attempted to lick away the juice. Her tongue moved indolently as if the sticky sweetness had paralyzed it. Michael emulated her, his tongue delicately licking her wrist. Her pulse went wild.

She was mesmerized by the rapid rise and fall of his chest. She placed her hand over his heart and felt its fierce pounding. Strong and vital, his heartbeat pulsed against her palm, drumming out a cadence of building desire.

Driven by a need to be closer still, Ashley slid her fingers between two of his shirt buttons, feeling skin, hair, heat.

Michael clapped his hand over hers and held it there, hard. But suddenly he grimaced and thrust her hand away, tossing a napkin into her lap and saying hoarsely, "For God's sake, Ash. Use that, if you don't want me all over you right here on the deck!"

She snatched the cloth and pressed it to her mouth as if stanching a wound. Her fingers shook, her entire body throbbed. She stared across the river to the Wisconsin shoreline until she felt calm enough to look at him again. The resolve she read in his eyes was clear: he might not be all over her, but he was going to kiss her—at last.

He approached slowly, keeping their gazes meshed. "I wanted to do this that first day, in the hotel lobby. And every minute since. I'm obsessed with your mouth."

All signs of hesitancy vanished when their lips touched. He dampened hers, his tongue gentle but insistent until her lips parted to admit him.

A breathy sigh escaped Ashley's throat, becoming lost in Michael's kiss. His hand rested on her waist and she grasped his arms to steady herself against the strange weakness spreading through her. His relentless seeking continued until he'd explored every secret her mouth offered; then he silently urged her to learn his just as intimately.

Her tongue slipped in, found his taste warm, sweet, drugging. The latent passion that had been building for days flared quickly, sweeping them into a spiral.

Within minutes, Ashley's prudent, career-woman persona resurfaced to issue a warning. She dragged her mouth from his. "We have to stop. I don't want this."

"You don't want— Then, lady, you're sending out the wrong signals."

His mouth claimed hers again, this time with less gentleness, less finesse. Bent on exposing the fragility of her protest, he didn't temper his demands until she yielded.

Her lips parted; her body relaxed. Ashley hadn't really believed that anyone, particularly herself, could be transported by a kiss. Only after he'd broken away did she realize how completely she had surrendered.

"Now tell me you didn't like that," Michael challenged.

"Don't you understand? I liked it too much. That's the problem."

His expression softened and his index finger trailed along her chin. "Honey," he told her with a rueful smile, "that's not a problem. I'd start worrying if you *didn't* like it."

"Please don't joke about this. I'm serious, Michael. I thought I could handle it. I see that I was wrong."

"What do you mean, 'handle it'?"

"Ignore the fact that, unbelievable as it is, you seem to want me."

"Of course, I want you, Ash," he said, his thumb and forefinger tipping up her chin. "Why should you try to ignore it?"

"Because my job is the most important thing in my life right now. There's no way I'm going to do anything to jeopardize it." She scooted to the edge of the quilt, hoping that the distance would provide some measure of safety. "In short, peddle your sexy wares elsewhere."

His body tensed with a fiery and sudden anger. She dreaded what he was about to say. Just as suddenly, he relaxed and his eyes warmed with that familiar, hungry glint. "I'm not peddling anything, and I'm damn sure not taking what I'm offering anywhere else."

"And I'm damn sure not interested in throwing away my future to scratch a random itch."

He groaned. Frustration and amusement merged in his voice. "Ashley Atwood, if you have any kind of itch, I'm the man who'll be scratching it."

4

MICHAEL GRIPPED THE PHONE more tightly and swiveled his chair around so he couldn't look through the curtains. He needed to listen to his caller's instructions, but watching Ashley at work sent his attention span to hell and back. He was scheduled to speak at next month's meeting of an Edina business organization, and he believed in being prepared.

Prepared. He had prepped himself for an internal audit, never expecting that the auditor, one Ashley Atwood, would present him with a perplexing personal dilemma—and not a financial moot point. Michael had been recruited by WTS straight out of college. Flexible as he was, one rule had remained unaltered in all those years: Never look twice at a woman you might find yourself working with, or for.

Until Ashley, he had scarcely been tempted to break his rule. Now he couldn't seem to stop himself. The obsessive attention Michael paid her wasn't simply because he found her attractive, though that factor wasn't to be discounted. Mainly he observed her trying to decide which identity was really Ashley. He opted for the daring firebrand he'd discovered in the flooded parking lot. Her reckless confrontation with a stranger who weighed twice as much as she did had captivated him. He couldn't get the scene out of his head. On the other hand, Ashley was doing her best to make him forget it. She desperately wanted to present the image of an emotionally detached, controlled professional.

After the Sunday they had spent on the boat, she had reverted to her role of bean-counting drudge. For five days she'd shown up wearing blah-colored suits and crisp blouses, with her hair rigidly contained in a mousy little bun perched on the back of her head. He almost expected her to poke a pencil into it to complete the prim caricature. There was no indication of her sense of humor, no hint of vibrancy in her personality. Surrounded by stacks of documents, she worked zealously at her computer, filling the spreadsheets with figures.

He finished his call, continuing to stare out his window. As diligently as she was trying, Ashley hadn't convinced him the woman he'd encountered first was the aberration. He kept looking for evidence of her vivacious alter ego, because that lady was warm and witty, likable and fun; someone he wanted to be with. The cool, efficient automaton next door left him feeling uneasy and rejected.

Instead of the warm greeting he had expected first thing Monday morning, Ashley had sent him the signal that she was in the audit "mode" and not to be interrupted. If she talked to him at all, it was in response to a direct question, each answer given succinctly and designed to eliminate the need for any further inquiry. After a few days of that, he was ready to bail out.

Then he recalled the ease with which they had communicated that first day, and on Sunday when her guard had dropped. Those memories reassured him that he'd been granted a glimpse of the true self that she worked so industriously to keep hidden. "Closeness" was an overworked term, but he couldn't think of a better one to describe what he and Ashley had shared on his houseboat. That wasn't all they'd shared.

The kiss. He slowly replayed it and his body grew inflamed from a sudden rush of heat—something that had become a disturbingly frequent sensation. No matter how steadfastly she tried to pretend it never happened, he wasn't going to let her forget the extraordinary moment when the accountant vanished and Ashley let her feelings take over, leaving them both shaken and clinging to each other.

The promise of her underlying warmth enticed him enough to grant him the patience to wait until Ashley's reticence again deserted her.

FOLLOWING A SATURDAY morning shopping trip to the mall, Ashley tucked a pair of waffle-soled athletic shoes and a Kelly-green jogging suit into her tote bag. During a late-night phone conversation, Michael had coaxed her into joining him for a day of "outdoor fun"—his description.

To Ashley, that sounded like a euphemistic way of sentencing her to physical exertion and bodily pain. One thing was certain: no matter how charming and persuasive he might be, she absolutely would not jog.

She also had to face another absolute—one that was much harder to deal with. All week she'd fought the good fight, suppressing her attraction to Michael. Her efforts had amounted to nothing. When he'd asked, she'd offered her prerequisite refusal before agreeing to go out with him. It was becoming apparent that she could only keep her distance from him for a limited amount of time. Then, like a danger junkie, she had to put herself at risk.

When she answered the door a short time later, Michael shook his head. Pointing at her pleated linen slacks and linen blouse, he teasingly inquired, "Chickening out on me?" He wore faded gray sweats that bore the maroon outlined-in-gold *M* of the University of Minnesota.

She had purposely dressed this way, hoping she might dissuade him from the planned outdoor activities. "I'll change later," she hedged. "After all, one simply can't parade around in public in a running suit." Damn! That line sounded prissy enough to do her mother proud.

He grinned. "It's the weekend, remember? One can dress any way one likes." He fingered the lace trim on the stand-up collar of her blouse. "Or do internal auditors always wear coordinated, starched outfits, even in bed?"

Ashley felt a blush inch up from her neck to her cheeks. It spread downward, too. Mercifully he couldn't see that. If he knew what she did or didn't wear to bed he wouldn't be so quick to pass judgment on her wardrobe. That wasn't a prudent topic for discussion, though it was as alive in his mind as in hers— or so his inviting look told her.

Her eyes widened as his fingers spread over the back of her waist, bringing her against him. "Keep them open, Ash, while I kiss you."

It happened so quickly. There was no initial testing of her receptiveness, no coaxing lead-in. Just his mouth on hers, warm and firm, filling her with his singular taste and texture.

She sighed, which he interpreted as an unconscious bid for him to take his fill—and he did, rediscovering the secrets of her mouth with a daring, intimate exploration. The wet friction of their tongues lightly brushing unleashed a tempest of sensations

Ashley had never felt before in *places* she'd never felt before. When he withdrew at last, she was trembling.

Lordy! The man could kiss. She'd have been content to stay in Michael's arms—which did not actually bode well for restraining her longings for him.

"You can hold me at bay all week, Ashley, armed with the prudish little suits and your incessant paper shuffling. But what you really want is there, simmering beneath the surface. You can't always prevent it from boiling over, can you?"

"Then I'll have to work at it, won't I?" Ashley bent to struggle with the zipper on her tote. She'd meant her statement to sound haughtier and more dismissive than it did. "Now, I believe I'm ready for that outdoor fun you promised."

His raised brows expressed skepticism.

"I thought we'd stop at my condo first," he told her on their way to Agnes. "It's a convenient place to park and you can change there before we go out to play." His smile was as expressive as his raised brows.

"Good!" Maybe she could fake an ankle sprain getting out of the Land Rover. Barring that, surely she could bluff her way through one day's action. She was curious to see his home, though it surprised her that he lived in a condo. A remodeled carriage house or old bungalow seemed more his style. She could even picture him on the third floor of a crumbling Victorian, like the one she rented in an old Atlanta neighborhood.

When they arrived at the complex, Ashley discovered her first guess had been close. His "condo" was in a converted grain silo in the heart of the city's lake district.

"Interesting," she remarked, admiring the sixth-story unit. It occupied two floors. Ashley crossed the graphite-colored carpet, drawn to expanses of glass that provided a view of the lakes and the downtown skyline.

Walls of exposed, rough-textured concrete and starkly simple furnishings created an indisputably masculine atmosphere. Two short, camel-colored leather couches faced each other, separated by an inlaid table. A single chair, a desk-bookcase combination and a piano were the only other pieces in the living room. In an adjoining dining area was a modern lacquered table with high-back chairs covered in camel-and-gray flame-stitch fabric.

"Unique, yet functional. I can see why you chose it."

"It suits me. When we moved here, my family bought a house in this part of town. I've always liked the area. Minneapolis is the only city I've lived in longer than two years, so it feels like home." He carried a grocery bag into the kitchen.

"Why did you move so often?" Through open shutters that separated the kitchen from the remainder of the downstairs, she watched Michael empty the bag and efficiently stow his purchases in white cabinets.

"My dad was an agent, and the FBI transfers its people often. Most assignments last about two years, so we were always changing schools. That's the main reason I decided to stay here and go to the U." He slid out a wine bottle from a built-in rack and put it in the refrigerator.

"A G-man! How exciting!" Ashley thought of her rather staid father and his lifelong association with a family's shipping business that was generations old. "It must have been difficult for the rest of the family to adjust to so many different places."

"Not really. We learned to be adaptable. Back then, Mom was great fun. She'd always play up the move as a big adventure. When the school year ended, we'd load up and strike out for unknown territory. Then we would spend all summer taking in the sights and discovering our new surroundings, like it was one long vacation."

"How clever. My mother sure isn't that amenable to change. She's spent her entire life in two houses."

Michael came back into the living room. "To me, it isn't where you are that's important, it's who you're with. Don't you agree?"

On the contrary. Ashley traveled to *avoid* being anywhere, with anyone, for too long. Since she'd never admitted that, even to Aunt Kitty, her closest confidante, she murmured in agreement.

"Why don't you change? I want to show you the neighborhood." He led her to the foot of an open staircase. "Bedrooms are up; choose either one."

She promised to be quick, stealing only a brief look at Michael's art as she climbed. Ashley came to an abrupt halt in the doorway of the first room. He could call it a "bedroom," but in her book, "torture chamber" would be a more apt term. She steered clear of his rowing machine and a stationary bike and nearly tripped over his weights.

She unbuttoned her blouse and opened the closet door to get a hanger. Ducking her head, she stepped back at once. The walk-in was crammed with sports equipment—downhill and cross-country skis and poles, hockey sticks, canoe paddles and life jackets, bow and arrows, golf clubs, fishing poles, ice and roller skates, scuba gear, tennis and assorted other rackets, snowshoes and a bowling ball. Even a sled. But not one hanger.

Her worst suspicions were confirmed. Michael wasn't your everyday garden-variety jock. He was a hard case.

His problem, she told herself on the way down the hall.

The second room was furnished with antiques. The burnished cherry four-poster, highboy and two bachelor chests were of excellent quality and quite old. Ashley wondered if they were more hand-me-downs. Why weren't they as stifling as the furnishings she'd grown up with? Being in Michael's bedroom disturbed her, so she hurriedly changed into her warm-up suit. Leaving her slacks and blouse neatly folded on his bed, she rushed back down.

"Hmm," he said, when she reached the bottom step. "I guess you're right."

"About what?"

He tugged her toward the windows. "Your eyes are green. They looked gray before. They're definitely green now. Must change color with what you wear."

Having him gaze at her with such intensity was an agitating reminder of what had happened earlier in her hotel room. She changed the subject. "Michael, do you use all that sports equipment?"

He shrugged. "I've used all of it at one time or another. I play a little tennis, swim, canoe and row during warm weather. In winter, I cross-country a couple of times a week on one of the lakes, swim at the club and do a few weights. My brother and I go diving in the Caymans every January. Other than that, I don't do much besides run."

Even worse than she'd imagined. There was no option except to tough it out. "What's our first stop?"

After his last speech, she was positive fun wasn't on today's program.

"We'll go around one of the lakes, either Cedar or Isles. Calhoun's closer. It's larger than the the other two."

He clearly expected her to protest. Ashley had no intention of complaining. Yet. "How far are we talking?"

"Both paths are roughly three miles. I can run them in about fifteen minutes."

Fifteen minutes to run! Let's try an all-day walk.

"We'll settle for a walk today so we can talk and enjoy the scenery. Walking is a good way to get in shape before you start a running program. You'd be surprised at what one or two miles a day will do for your conditioning."

"I'm sure I would be." Who was he kidding? Ashley was certain she must have walked that distance at some point in her life. Not in recent memory, however.

Strolling leisurely, they walked behind a group of town houses and across a railroad track to the public beach on Cedar Lake. The day was pleasantly warm, and bright with signs of spring all around. Trees were in varied stages of sprouting new leaves. Tulips and daffodils poked out of the thawed soil. Ducks and geese paddled close to shore, hoping some generous passerby would toss them bread crumbs or corn, and many did.

After keeping pace for about ten minutes, Ashley got a stitch in her right side. "Do you think we could slow down a little?"

He let up a bit. "We've only started. I can't believe you're out of breath so soon."

"Believe it," she snapped testily. She should never have agreed to an outing with a jock. Everyone knew they were sadists.

"You're in terrible shape." He examined her petite, slender figure with a cheeky grin. "Aerobically speaking, I mean."

"Naturally."

"What *do* you do for exercise?" he asked, slowing even more.

"Lift a fork every chance I get."

Michael stared at her in disbelief. "Surely you do something?"

"Stop trying to make me feel guilty for being a couch potato." Ashley halted and crossed her arms in front of her. "I," she informed him with a guileless smile, "do not believe in letting my pleasures kill me."

He looked astonished because, like most fitness freaks, he couldn't imagine anyone not getting off on a punishing exercise regimen. "I'm sure all you need is a basic program. It'll make you feel great."

"I feel fine now. I'm not overweight, my thighs don't applaud when I walk and my doctor assures me I'm in excellent health. My body's treated me okay so far. Why should I start beating up on it now?"

"But don't you think—"

"Let's just say I'm not into sweat." That ought to squelch the subject.

He grinned in a boyishly captivating way, getting in the last word. "I'll have you jogging yet, Ms. Atwood. Bet your Gucci's on it." Before Ashley could disagree, he pointed out the rack where he chained his canoe in the summer. "From here, you can paddle to three other connecting lakes. You'd like canoeing. It's very relaxing."

She detected the hint of a smirk, refusing to rise to his bait.

The paved path ended about halfway around the lake. Soon they were back in view of the condo and Ashley did feel more invigorated than tired. She reflected on that silently, unwilling to give Michael a chance to say "I told you so."

"How about lunch? I'll bet with all this exertion you've worked up quite an appetite."

"Don't press your luck, Jordan. There's still half a day left."

Michael laughed and pulled her close in a one-armed hug. "Come on, now. Confess. You loved every minute."

"I'd never own up to that. If I did, you might try to get me on those roller skates I saw upstairs."

"Not a chance. I haven't used them in years. Skating around Isles used to be fun before it got so trendy that I had to give it up. You can't imagine what a glorified human supermarket it's turned into, especially on weekends."

He took her by surprise with his challenge, "Last one to the elevator buys lunch."

Not one to refuse a dare, Ashley took off in a flash. The distance was short and she easily bested Michael, who was inexplicably slow. She knew he'd allowed her to win. It was hard to resent something that pleased him so much.

"See," he said with satisfaction. "I swore you'd be jogging, and you did."

"Oh." Ashley slapped her forehead. "I think I've been had."

His teasing dissolved in an instant and his voice turned husky. "Not yet, you haven't."

But his eyes promised: *Soon.*

FOLLOWING LUNCH AT his favorite grill, Michael announced his game plan: a bike ride around three lakes. Ashley voiced a token protest, and got on the ten-speed he'd borrowed from one of his neighbors. After she'd gamely pedaled through the proposed route without so much as a whimper, she suggested they take in a late-afternoon movie, and asked if they could return to his apartment so she could change out of her jogging suit and into pants and a blouse.

The old Art Deco theater he chose was made to order for *Wuthering Heights*. They bought snacks and Michael led her to seats high in the back of the deserted balcony.

"I didn't know there were any theaters left that had balconies," Ashley remarked, arranging a huge tub of popcorn on her lap.

Michael grinned. "Gotta preserve a few places for overheated teenagers and perverts." He tore open a box of chocolate mints and chucked one into his mouth.

"Of which you are neither," she said with mock sternness.

He popped another chocolate-coated candy. "You hope."

The lights dimmed and Ashley told herself she could relax for the next ninety minutes or so. Men like Michael didn't take women to movies and paw them in the darkness. They didn't need to. Such men had their pick of willing partners anytime they wanted one.

Before long, however, she wished she hadn't spent so much time brooding about that certainty. Michael wrapped his left arm around her shoulders.

"Want a mint?"

He must have mistaken the shake of her head for an affirmative, because his other hand reached across, plucked a mint from the box and touched it to her lips. Before she could shake her head again, he leaned close and laid it on his tongue, right in her line of vision.

Ashley tried not to watch, but his profile was so near, and she couldn't tear her gaze away. It was a simple act, really, taking in a small piece of candy. When it was Michael's mouth, however, the act was laden with sensual overtones.

"Sure?" he asked, and she could feel his moist breath on her ear, smell the rich chocolate and mint.

"Popcorn," she whispered, glad she didn't have to speak aloud and let him hear her voice crack. "I'll stick with that." Pretending absorption in the Coming Attractions, Ashley gobbled a handful of it as if she were starving.

He dropped the mint box and rested his candy-eating hand on her stomach. "Feed me some."

She stilled at the command. An image of them on the quilt on the deck of his boat superimposed itself on the screen. That day she'd been aware of the sublimal eroticism of Michael sliding every bite into her mouth. The prospect of doing the same for him now was enough to inspire carnal thoughts.

"Feed me, Ash," he repeated.

Her fingers shaking, she held a single piece to his lips and watched his teeth capture it. She meant to pull her hand away, but as before, when she was under the spell of Michael's voice and eyes, rational thought got suspended. She allowed his tongue to snake around her thumb and forefinger, lick off the butter, savoring the taste, and lick again.

Tremors sparked at the point of contact and raced to every part of her. Too late, Ashley's hand dropped to her lap. She hadn't the strength to hold it up, knew she'd never be able to raise it again because of the lethargy that claimed her. Yet, when Michael demanded "More," in his low and sexy way, she obeyed instinctively.

Each nibble he took deepened the spell, fed her fantasies, drove her desires into forbidden territory. This time, when he gave her fingers a warm bath, she gave no thought to withdrawing. Knowing that being here, allowing Michael to sweep her away, was insanity of the first order, she still offered herself up to frenzy of the moment.

The popcorn tumbled to the floor, unnoticed. He took her mouth completely then, initiating a deep, thrusting rhythm that Ashley welcomed without reservation. Every time they kissed, all was flaming turbulence. And this was no different; neither of them could taste enough, touch enough. And the scent of Ashley's perfume rose, its light floral fragrance changed by their combined heat into something headier, earthier.

Ashley and Michael wrenched apart at the same moment. His stunned look mirrored hers. He had been just as out of control as she, making her feel only marginally better about behaving with such abandon.

She groped beside her feet for her cup of cola to cool herself off. She vowed to get her mind back on the movie. After a series of reviving swallows she extended the container to him. "Drink?"

He nodded, his gaze holding hers hostage. Spellbound, she watched his mouth open, his tongue curl around the straw and, when he began to suck on it, the slow, measured flex of his cheeks made her breasts feel unbearably heavy—tingling with arousal, aching to be touched.

"Tell me what you want, Ash," he whispered, reading her thoughts as easily as he finished the cola. "Never mind. I know."

Michael's lips centered on the wild pulse beating in the hollow of her throat while his hand closed over her breast in the gentlest of possessive gestures. His palm smoothed and stroked, over and over.

"These stiff, prim blouses—you wear them like armor, as if they can keep anyone from guessing what's underneath." His hand moved to her other breast and squeezed lightly, finding silent proof that the disguise hadn't fooled him. "You know what, Ash? To a man who's interested, observant, you give yourself away. Every time."

She wanted to pull back. His inflaming touch diminished her willpower.

"Pleats, a little bit of lace, a ruffle—they all scream 'Look at me! I'm a woman!' Well, I've looked, and I've seen. I want you."

Her skin came alive—not only her breasts but her entire body. She twisted in her seat, yearning for him with frightening recklessness.

"Want to know what drives me wild? Those tiny buttons on that light gray thing you wear. A row of them on each shoulder, that trails down to..." His little finger grazed over her nipple, touching it so softly she might have imagined it if he hadn't returned to draw circles around the almost painfully taut crest. "If I were to undo all of them one by one, then my lips, my tongue could be here," Ashley arched her head back, picturing his mouth there, sensing the wet, pulling pressure, and she couldn't stop herself from moaning.

He made a sound against her neck before she felt her skin there being drawn into the searing heat of his mouth. At the same time, his thumb and forefinger tugged at the sensitive peak, making it harder while he whispered that her responsiveness was making him hard, too.

She was damp all over, throbbing inside, breathless. "Oh, Michael. What are you doing to me?"

"Making love to you . . . in my mind. I've taken my time, made you hot and wet, like I am right now." He went on to tell her what was about to happen to him as a result of his imaginings, and Ashley was inundated by a wave of heat, swamping her with its force.

She was in too deep. "Michael, we have to stop this."

"You're all I think about," he groaned. His hand swept the entire length of her body. "Let's get out of here. I have to be alone with you."

"But the movie—"

"I've seen it. Several times."

So had Ashley, and she bent to gather up their trash.

"Wanna check and see if there's any ice left in that cup?"

She rattled the container. "A little. Why?"

"I think you'd better pour it in my lap so I'll be able to walk out of here."

"It's your own fault," she told him with a lift of her chin. "I'm not the one responsible for turbocharging your libido."

He laughed loudly enough to turn a few heads below them. "If you can say that with a straight face, you deserve whatever happens to you."

"We rarely get what we deserve."

"Tell me about it. At the moment I am the world's foremost authority on not getting what I deserve."

A charged stillness blanketed them as they walked to the parking lot. Ashley knew they were both thinking the same thing. *Where do we go from here?* She imagined that Michael would phrase the question quite simply; "Your place or mine?" She was twisted in a Gordian knot of conscience, and self-condemnation. Their interlude in the balcony terrified her. Ashley felt like her life was careening out of control.

It would be impossible to take charge of it again if they ended up at his condo or her hotel. It would be so easy to give in, because she desperately desired to make love with Michael. Even if it were only one time, the prospect tantalized her. She would not succumb. On the balance sheet, a few minutes of temporary ecstasy could never outweigh the years she had spent carefully constructing a life of her own.

"All right, Ash," Michael said when they stopped beside his car. "Let's have it."

"Have what?"

"The excuses you've manufactured. I could almost hear wheels turning the moment we left the theater."

She had expected him to come on hot and heavy the instant they were alone. Instead, he was lightening the mood. "Not excuses, exactly."

"No? I figured your brain's in a mad scramble to come up with a couple dozen reasons why we shouldn't carry our love scene to its logical conclusion."

"Men are *so literal!*" she grumbled, wondering when she'd become an authority on the male of the species.

"Can't be helped. It's in our genes, or something." He bent to unlock her door. "So, where shall we go to keep our idle hands from doing the devil's work?"

Out of relief, Ashley smiled. "You know that cemetery we rode by earlier, the one up on a hill?"

"Why, Miz Scarlett, are you telling me you want to go parking in a cemetery? In the dark?"

She laughed at his travesty of a Southern accent. "Sometimes that's when it's best."

"It? Sounds kinky."

"Not unless you consider hunting epitaphs kinky. I've collected them all over the world. That's what I do in my spare time."

He studied her in the reflected glow of the car's overhead light. Then he nodded and gave her nose a quick, playful peck.

"You're on. And while we're at it, maybe we can lay that saintly accountant, Ms. Atwood, to rest."

5

ASHLEY LET OUT a huge sigh the minute she closed her hotel-room door behind Michael. Ever since they had left the theater, she'd been holding her breath in anticipation that he would attempt another seduction. To sidestep that, she'd impulsively divulged one of her quirks. Ashley the accountant would never propose a spur-of-the-moment epitaph hunt. And yet, after assessing her and the idea thoroughly, Michael had gone along with the suggestion.

She couldn't believe a man would shift from the throes of passion to the outrageousness of an escapade so easily and agreeably. Since he had, she wasn't going to test her luck.

They'd spent the next two hours dashing around a dark cemetery, reading inscriptions on tombstones by flashlight, laughing and playing like two naughty children. He'd been the one to discover a "keeper" for her extensive collection; they had both cracked up when Michael called her over and read one deceased's parting shot: "I Told You I Was Sick."

Afterward, they had eaten at a coffee shop near her hotel and Michael had left her at the door with a

brotherly kiss on the cheek. "Everything we did today was fun, Ashley," he had told her. "Think about
that when you go to put on your suit and stiff-necked
blouse Monday morning."

Dead certain that she was on a collision course
heading toward romantic and professional disaster,
Ashley felt compelled to call her Aunt Kitty. At all the
crisis points in her life, she had turned to her. Katherine Atwood would never make decisions for her;
instead, she provided a rare combination of objectiv-
ity and support that always helped Ashley to make up
her own mind. She recalled how Kitty's wise level-
headedness had provided her with the resolve to defy
her mother's expectations for her, and the courage to
fulfill her own.

Ashley remembered the day of her high-school
graduation. She was in a dither over the dress her
mother was insisting she wear to the event. . . .

"DO YOU BELIEVE this dress?" Ashley fumed. She
grabbed a handful of the lace-trimmed white or-
ganza. "I look like a Barbie doll in her wedding cos-
tume. All this froufrou for a tea dance at the country
club."

Wearing a fashionable two-piece yellow knit from
a French designer, Kitty smiled in sympathy. "That's
our Ellie. Her daughter is going to dress like a refined
Southern lady, or there'll be hell to pay."

Ashley laughed. Her mother deplored being called Ellie. "Then I hope she looks long and hard at me today. Because this is the last time she'll see me wearing something she picked out."

"What about shopping for a college wardrobe? I'm sure she has that penciled in on her calendar."

"Well, she's going to be disappointed, not to mention furious." Ashley turned serious. "You see, I'm not going to attend the college of her choice, so I won't be needing her wardrobe, either."

"Bully for you!" Kitty exclaimed. "I never could see you at Sweet Briar, anyway."

"Talk about hell to pay when Mother hears I'm shunning her alma mater. I think she must have enrolled me the day we got home from the hospital. But I've made up my mind about this, and I won't be swayed."

"Do you have an alternative plan?"

"You bet I do. I applied to the University of Michigan months ago, and they've accepted me. Come September, I'll be a Yankee."

Kitty led her to the window seat and they sat side by side. "Ashley, I'm glad to see you start making your own decisions. Are you doing this for yourself or merely to defy your mother?"

She started to protest, then thoughtfully considered her aunt's question. She conceded, "Maybe it's a little of both. All I know is that I have to get away from here. I'll never be what Mother wants or expects. Even if I spent the rest of my life trying, I'd fail miserably at being some man's Mrs. And I wouldn't do any better playing society matron. The only solution is to put as much distance as possible between me and Mother's expectations."

"You certainly eliminated proximity when you picked Michigan," Kitty said wryly. "Aren't you afraid of freezing your little Southern derriere?"

"I'm afraid, period." She grabbed the older woman's hand. "I wish I were strong and independent and confident, like you."

"Shoot, honey," Kitty urged, squeezing Ashley's fingers. "Do you think I started out this way?" She nodded at Ashley's startled look. "I was just as confused about what and who I wanted to be as you are right now."

"So, how did you turn out so sophisticated and successful?"

"I know it sounds simplistic, but you have to ask yourself, 'What do I want out of life?' When you decide what that is, then work toward it. One morning you'll wake up and realize that you are who you wanted to be."

Ashley licked her lips, nervous about asking her aunt a private question. "What were your goals, Kitty?"

"Nothing all that exalted, really. I needed to know I could take care of myself. I felt the best way to ensure that was by starting my own advertising agency so I'd have control. And I wanted to be happy."

"Are you happy?" Ashley asked. "Is your independent life a good one?"

Kitty looked deeply into her niece's eyes. "All I can tell you, Ashley, is that it's been right for me. I can't guarantee the same will be true for you. I will promise this: you can be anything you set your mind to. I always believed I had this capability to take charge of my life and mold it into whatever I wished it to be. You have that capacity as much as I do. Use it."

"I'm going to," Ashley whispered. "Starting today."

KITTY HAD BEEN Ashley's lodestar. She had chosen accounting chiefly because she couldn't envision her mother or sister excelling in that field. By some miracle she was not only good at it, she truly liked it. And she'd built a satisfying though somewhat singular existence based on her career. Like her aunt, she had convinced herself she was happy.

Now, for the first time ever, she was wavering. Never had she felt so strongly in need of Kitty's advice. She dialed Kitty's home number in New York.

When the ringing continued unanswered, Ashley dropped the handset in its cradle. She felt bereft and isolated. Usually Kitty's absence wouldn't have been this disturbing. Her aunt had an active business and social schedule. Going out on weekends with her many friends was the norm for her. This time, Ashley felt increasingly desperate.

She phoned twice more before giving up and going to bed. On Sunday, she continued to try at regular intervals. By late that night when her aunt still hadn't returned home, Ashley decided she must have gone out of town on business—something else she did often. It had been such a long day of solitary contemplation, and the end result was a reinforcement of her pressing need for reassurance from Kitty. Without fail, tomorrow she had to track down her elusive relative.

ASHLEY GLARED at the green numbers on her computer screen. Yet again, she'd made a transposition error.

It was Monday morning. That's why she was having trouble concentrating. Of course, she'd had the same trouble yesterday. She might as well be honest with herself and place the blame squarely where it belonged.

Michael Jordan was the cause of her distraction. Until she could get in touch with Aunt Kitty and use her as a sounding board, Ashley knew her worried preoccupation wouldn't be alleviated. When she broke for lunch, she was going to be on the horn to New York.

Optimistic that she'd soon have some heartening advice, Ashley directed her fingers over the computer keyboard with renewed determination. She would not peer into the office next door one more time—not even surreptitiously—to check if Michael had finally appeared. She was going to keep herself so busy he couldn't intrude in any way. At least her poor judgment concerning him—seeing him outside work—hadn't kept the audit from progressing smoothly. If she could prevent Michael from distracting her anymore, they might be able to finish ahead of schedule and make an early exit. Beginning this afternoon, she'd attempt to squeeze overtime shifts out of Jack and Mark. Let them complain all they liked. Anything was preferable to the ominous feeling of being stalked.

Her good intentions sustained her concentration for almost two hours.

"Morning, Ms. Atwood." The way he said her name sounded faintly accusatory. "You have a pleasant Sunday?"

Just dandy, you cocky jock. He needn't know her day had dragged interminably, or that she'd spent it wallowing in confusion and guilt. Without glancing up, she recorded a figure on the screen. "Very nice, thank you."

"Saturday was nicer."

Her head snapped up at the quiet, unmistakable seductiveness of his tone. She looked around, hoping to see Jack or Mark riding to her rescue. She could only blame herself that they were nowhere in sight. She'd sent both off in search of some missing invoices.

Michael closed the door, insulating them against curious ears in the outer office. "It's been years since I did any heavy petting in a dark balcony. Now I remember why I never went in for it much. Too frustrating." He passed her a pained look, as if she were personally responsible for his condition. "Did you know, Ashley, that when a man wants one particular woman, the usual alternative isn't . . . satisfying? You can try, but it doesn't put out the fire."

She gaped at him. He'd changed the rules. She was now fair game at the office. "Are you crazy?" she hissed. "Have you forgotten where we are?"

"It's not likely you'd ever let me forget." Michael sat down across from Ashley, fully aware that he wasn't playing by the rules. The uncertainty of their relationship had eaten at him until he couldn't see any solution except direct attack. He had to prove to himself that the woman he wanted more every day was someone who was fundamentally warm and nurturing, open to people and experiences. To love. He couldn't accept having such powerful feelings, such an unrelenting desire, for a cold, calculating female who cared about nothing aside from advancing her career.

His mother's unwavering dedication to her accounting firm was alienating her husband and destroying her marriage. Michael wasn't about to get himself trapped in that kind of dead-end relationship. So he saw no choice except to force the issue. "Did slamming the door in my face Saturday night leave you as restless and agitated as it did me?"

Ashley wondered if he was doing this to get back at her. Did he think her the worst kind of tease? "I didn't slam the door in your face," she said, evading his real question.

"Figuratively."

"Michael, this can't go any further."

"Why?"

"Isn't it obvious?"

"No."

His quiet one-word sentences unnerved her more than an angry tirade. "This is not—"

"During the movie you wanted it to go a lot further. Your body was telling me plenty, and it wasn't lying. You were as ready as I was."

She straightened in her chair. "What do you want from me?" Ashley brought her ruler down with a crack. "I've already admitted it and I'll say it again. There's chemistry between us."

He didn't even waste a word on that, voicing his opinion with a snort.

"Don't you see?" she persisted. "Physical attraction is the worst possible reason to get involved." The hysterical note that had crept into her voice wouldn't help her plead her case.

"Hardly the worst," he disagreed, unbuttoning his jacket as if he intended to stay awhile. "On the other hand, it isn't the only reason to get involved, though it seems that way at the beginning, when everything is so intense."

She'd been staring at the screen, but now looked up into his eyes. Talk about intense. "Still, that's the only basis you and I have for an . . . uh . . ."

He shook his head at her inability to say the word. "If you're telling me that all we have going for us is the physical thing, then I'm telling you that's so much horse manure."

"Michael, I'm trying to make it clear that I don't indulge in random sexual encounters."

"I never thought you did. Neither do I. Morality aside, these days it could be suicidal."

"You're not taking me seriously," she accused.

"What do you expect? First you call me a random itch, then a random sexual encounter." He spread both hands on the table between them, his fingers long and brown and beguiling. "I am not a random kind of man, Ashley. Maybe you need to get that straight in your head."

That was the trouble. It was already straight in her head what kind of man Michael was. The dangerous kind. "This isn't a typical meet-chat-mate syndrome," she protested. It was vital that she base her argument on logical, concrete factors rather than emotional variables. Except, at the moment, logic escaped her. She felt extremely emotional "There are issues here, such as conflict of interest, that make it impossible for us to get involved."

He rolled his eyes. "Give me a break. You have to stretch pretty far to get conflict of interest out of this situation." When she opened her mouth he cut off her argument. "Granted, you're auditing my division, but there's nothing to hang me with there. You'll end up with a clean report and neither of us will be compromised."

"You sound very certain that I won't find any irregularities." She gave him her chilliest smile. "I guess my reputation didn't precede me."

An answering smile, infinitely warmer than hers, flitted across his face. "Oh, yes. I've heard all about you. Oliver, at headquarters, got a real buzz out of informing me it was my turn to take on the Killer Mole."

"Then if I were you, I'd heed the warning and think twice about tangling with an internal auditor. It might get you in deeper than you want to go."

He winked. The man actually had the nerve to wink at her in the office! Ashley was appalled. Incensed.

"Honey, I've thought—a lot more than twice—about tangling with you." He stood, hands in his pockets, pushing aside his dignified pin-striped jacket, a stodgy counterpoint to his sexual allusion. "If that gets me in deep, I'll just have to take my punishment like a man."

She jumped to her feet so abruptly the papers scattered in all directions. She barely noticed. "Mr. Jordan, this conversation is unprofessional and unacceptable. If you have nothing more pressing on your calendar than harassing a co-worker, I suggest you take the rest of the day off."

Shaking with fury, Ashley fled the room. By the time she reached the car, she was already regretting her dramatic exodus. There was no changing that now.

She was livid that Michael had provoked her to react with such fury. It rankled that he had so much power over her. Why did she allow him to get to her? By what means could she counter him?

What was her forte? It certainly wasn't dealing with men like Michael. The only thing she felt confident and accomplished in was her accounting skills. They weren't much help in her present plight. Or were they?

Her brows drew together as she mulled over the accounting principle of offsetting entries. With a little luck and the discovery of an offsetting entry to put Michael in his place—at a safe distance from her—she might be able to regain the advantage she'd lost in this morning's skirmish with him.

She found her rental car in the lot and decided to calm herself down by going for a long drive. After a couple of angry stabs, she managed to cram the key into the ignition and start the engine. She drove out of the parking lot with exaggerated care, mindful that all her troubles had begun with an accident in this very lot.

When she returned, her offsetting-entry strategy was in place. It wasn't ideal, but every additional confrontation with Michael made self-preservation a higher priority.

Michael had told her, with a touch of arrogance, she'd find nothing to hang him with. Maybe not, but it wouldn't be because she gave less than a hundred percent to the task. From now on, she was going to pour every bit of her energy and concentration into the audit. She was going to play the role of Killer Mole to the hilt. Let him dare to say one more offensive word. She was ready. In fact, she couldn't wait to freeze him with indifference.

Instead, she had to seethe in silence for the rest of the day. The hound had left a snide little note attached to her computer screen. It read, "Nothing pressing on my calendar, so I'm taking your advice. See you tomorrow."

She crushed it into a tight ball, but the message rang in her head for hours.

AFTER INSISTING Jack and Mark put in three excessively long days, Ashley let them go at six o'clock on Thursday. All week they'd been giving her strange looks, and she knew they were bound to ask questions if she didn't ease up. A relaxing evening would have been impossible, given the circumstances, so she remained at the office. Late that afternoon she had picked up the first inkling of trouble with the audit. As yet, she'd found nothing specific to base her suspicions on; nonetheless, her instincts had proved reliable too often in the past. It was time to let them take over.

For more than two hours she worked alone, tuning out the booming thunder and wicked lightning of another spring storm. Ashley still hadn't found the obscure clue she needed, when she suddenly heard footsteps nearing the conference room. Her heart speeded up. Emerging from the darkened office, Michael leaned against the doorframe, his arms crossed, watching her with unconcealed hunger. She felt like an outclassed general facing a superior opponent.

"You shouldn't sneak up that way," she scolded. Her pulse thudded, and not because he'd startled her.

He didn't move. "A sneak attack is probably the only way I'm gong to breach your defenses." He lifted one shoulder. "I'll use whatever it takes."

His resonant voice ruffled her composure. She figured he had already guessed her defenses were marginal at best; that they could be penetrated by the mere fact of his presence.

He'd gone home to change and now wore the navy pants with white side-stripes she had seen before. Tonight, her attention was riveted on the lone coppery button at his waist. Ashley had the foolhardy compulsion to unsnap it. She moved both hands to her lap, out of sight.

She didn't believe he'd read her mind, but Michael hooked a thumb in his waistband and fingered the button. Innocently? Suggestively? "Are you ready, Ashley?" His eyes, dark with passion, drew hers upward so their gazes clashed.

"Ready?" Her voice came out faint, whispery. She couldn't look away.

After a tension-building interval when the only sound was the storm overhead, he answered. "To leave. It's past eight and you haven't had dinner. Aren't you hungry?"

"No! Are you?"

"Yeah."

Ashley quivered at the degree of need he could pack into one quiet word. He didn't want dinner any more than she did. They both wanted the same thing. Since she was the one who knew that shouldn't happen, she once again had to suppress her insane desire for him. She wished it was easier to find the words, and say them convincingly.

"Michael, we have to settle this right now."

"I agree. That's the reason I tracked you down tonight."

His agreement was anything but encouraging. "I'm sure our ideas of how to solve the problem differ radically."

He shifted positions and his gaze narrowed. "No doubt mine is too simple, too direct for you."

She cleared her throat and sat up a little straighter, determined to survive this with her poise intact. "I'm here on an assignment. Dodging innuendos from a division vice president is not in the job description. If you persist, I'll have no choice except to retaliate." Ashley hadn't a clue how she'd back up her threat.

"Is that the whole speech?"

She felt her teeth start to grind and forced her jaws to relax. Why wouldn't he listen to what she said and admit the truth of it? "My *speech* addressed a legitimate concern."

He smiled a little at her stilted reply. "A legitimate concern in most cases. This is different."

"I don't see how."

"You do. You're just determined to deny it. What's going on between us isn't about business at all. Yet you continue wielding the audit like a sword to keep me at arm's length. I think you know by now it isn't going to work. You might as well give up."

Ashley was enough of a realist to concede his point, though it was a bitter pill to swallow. If Michael wanted to approach this from the personal angle, she had an equally valid argument.

"Let's suppose, for the sake of discussion, that I willingly hop into bed with you tonight. Say we're insatiable, and we do it again tomorrow evening, and the next, as well." She paused, and though she had his attention, he looked too engrossed in her hypothetical scenario to speak. "Let's even go so far as to say we spend every night together until the job is finished."

"It's a start," he agreed in a voice turned suddenly hoarse.

"Exactly. And that's all it would ever be, since we both know I'll be leaving soon. Minneapolis is just a stop along the way for me, like anywhere else. I would be begging for misery if I got caught up in a fling so brief it wouldn't even deserve to be called an affair." He didn't appear nearly as swayed by her oratory as she was. "Surely you understand why I steer clear of an involvement that's doomed from the beginning."

"Well, Ash, what you've said makes a certain amount of sense. Hypothetically speaking, that is."

"But?" She wasn't going to like his answer. He looked far too optimistic.

"I don't buy a word of this excuse, either." He turned away, as if he hadn't just taken the wind out of her sails. "I had some of my people track down those order-entry forms Jack couldn't find earlier. I'll get them for you."

Ashley directed her muddled senses to the working papers in front of her. Piles of paper were a flimsy barricade against the onslaught of Michael's sexuality. His body, his voice . . . she was worn out from trying to resist him.

She'd been sitting in this chair for close to fourteen hours with hardly a break, and she was shaky with exhaustion. No wonder she was susceptible to Michael at this point. Any woman would be. In a minute she'd go to the phone in the corner and dial a cab. Back at her hotel she would order a drink and the most expensive entrée on the room-service menu, then soak in a hot bath. After a good night's sleep she'd again be armed and ready. This was one battle she couldn't afford to let Michael win.

She knew exactly what she ought to do, and her plan seemed sensible and workable, until he deposited a thick manila folder in front of her. He lowered himself into a chair with the fluid runner's grace that Ashley wished she didn't find so attractive. Propping both feet on the table, he crossed them at the ankles and rested a mug at the juncture of his legs. She couldn't help it—her gaze instantly homed in on that one place she should not be looking. When she read the message on the mug's side, she muffled a groan. Divers Do It Deeper.

Awash in erotic sensations, she stared as Michael slowly circled the mug's rim with his middle finger. Her heart took up its now familiar wild pumping, sending tremors all through her body.

"You must get tired, spending so much time and effort stifling your reactions to me."

"What reactions?" It was bad enough to be inarticulate at a time like this; worse, still, to croak like a bullfrog. Whereas his voice poured over her like sweet, flowing honey.

"Your mouth. It's dry." His tongue washed over his lips. "So dry you can hardly swallow."

Ashley experimented. His guess was so accurate it was almost painful. "Michael, don't talk like this. Not now."

"That's not the worst, is it? The worst is that heavy ache, deep and low . . . where you want me to be."

He rubbed a thumb back and forth across his lower lip until Ashley was on the verge of screaming in frustration. She didn't dare move; yet she couldn't sit still.

"Face it, Ash," he said, raking her with a bold look, "if you're trying to conceal your responses, you ought to wear something other than silk."

Mute, she saw as well as felt her body's betrayal. Defying the layers of camisole and blouse, her nipples stood out. "Please don't do this to me. Please," she whispered, hating the thought that she'd beg him for anything, hating that it would do no good.

"All right." He sighed, sitting forward. "This is torturing both of us. You know where I stand. I've had it with pressure tactics." He rose and stuffed his hands into his front pockets. "Tomorrow afternoon I'm heading up to my family's lake house. I want you to come with me. I think if we can spend some together, get to know each other without work interfering, we can—"

He broke off, leaving Ashley to ponder if he might be as ambivalent, as confused about what he wanted, as she was. "I don't know if—"

"This is the only time I'll ask. And I promise not to argue with your decision. You're a big girl now. I'd like to think you have the guts to take what you want."

Ashley would like to think she had guts, too. All she had to do was say no one more time and she had Michael's word he wouldn't push her. His capitulation was like an answered prayer because it would be easy to refuse the invitation. Not in this lifetime would she go away with a man who had so much power over her.

"I'll let you know in the morning." She took the cowardly way out, assuming it would be easier to give him her answer when they were surrounded by witnesses.

"Come on, then," he said, moving to the door. "I'll drop you off at the hotel."

Too weary to argue, Ashley shut off her computer and followed.

Inside the elevator they stood on opposite sides, much as two strangers do when forced to share a confined space. The building had only two stories. Before they reached the first floor, the elevator jerked to a halt and they were plunged into total darkness.

"Oh, great!" Ashley remarked in disgust. "This is all I need."

The only sound was a guttural "God, no! Not now! I can't! Why?"

"Michael, are you okay?" When there was no reply, she asked, "Does this sort of thing happen often? Will we be stuck here long?"

Still no response. "Michael?"

Silence. Overwhelming blackness. "Michael, say something!"

She heard him breathing heavily. His labored pants were an unmistakable sign of terror.

Ashley set down her briefcase and slowly felt her way along the elevator's handrail toward him. "Michael, can you tell me what's wrong?"

He tried to speak. It came out choked and incoherent. After several more garbled attempts, she made out part of a word. "Pho— Phob—" He gave up after two tries.

"Claustrophobia," she repeated, confirming her suspicion. "A dark elevator is the worst place in the world to be, isn't it?" She didn't expect him to reply. Right now she only wanted him to listen to her, concentrate on her soothing voice. "I understand what you're going through, believe me. I'm a recovered phobic, and I can show you a simple exercise that helped me."

His only answer was a strangled moan. It was still pitch black around them and Ashley knew that even if their eyes adjusted, they wouldn't be able to see each other. There was simply no source of light anywhere. They'd have to rely on touch. Tentatively she reached out to him, found a shoulder and traced it down to his fist, which had a stranglehold on the metal rail. She disengaged it with gentle firmness and said, "Flex and extend your fingers. Try to relax them." Her hand closed over his to demonstrate.

She could feel the heat pouring off him. Her hands were cool so she placed them on the sides of his neck. Michael's pulse pounded frantically against her palms. "Now, we're going to breathe together. Slow and deep. Inhale . . . hold it as long as you can, then exhale. Do it just like I am. In. And out."

She kept him practicing for a couple of minutes, but couldn't detect any slowing of his heart rate. "Put your fingers on the pulse point below my ear. That way you can measure the beats." She wasn't sure if he heard her, or was able to obey. At last his hand came up, grazing her breast for a fleeting moment before finding the spot on her neck. She knew Michael wasn't aware of where he'd touched her, but warmth suffused her. "In. And out. Again."

He struggled to follow orders. His first few breaths sounded as if they might be his last breaths. Ashley breathed steadily, continuing to coach him, and gradually Michael's respiration began to calm a bit. She didn't know how long they'd be trapped. If she had to instruct him all night, she would. She had her own frightening memories of how paralyzing fear like this could be.

What seemed like an hour in darkened captivity was in reality no more than ten minutes. The lights winked on, off, on again, and stayed. The elevator shuddered, and within seconds the door whooshed open at the parking-garage level. Neither of them moved.

He still needed her. Instinctively Ashley wrapped her arms around his waist and held him in a snug embrace. She touched him, her hands swirling over his back in circles while she murmured repeated reassurances.

At last Michael sucked in a huge breath and returned her embrace. "Thank you," he said softly. "It's dumb, irrational fear, and I know it. I can't control it. I become catatonic when the closed space is dark. Otherwise I can handle the claustrophobia fairly well."

"Phobias may be irrational, but they're frighteningly real all the same. Sometime I'll tell you all about how I learned not to be petrified of flying. It'll work for you, too."

He pulled back just enough for her to see his smile. It was so genuine, so grateful, so sweet, that she felt her breath hitch in her throat.

"I'll never forget this, Ashley. What you did... having you with me was a lifesaver."

She smiled back. Later the realization struck her that she'd given him a great deal more than help with his phobia.

In return, he'd stolen her only real defense.

6

THE CLICHÉ, "tension so thick you could cut it with a knife," must have been born under conditions like this, Ashley thought, crossing and uncrossing her legs for the third time. She and Michael had exited a diner after a strained, silent lunch where they'd left their sandwiches uneaten on the plates. They stopped at her hotel to pick up her overnight bag.

Last night, Michael had unleashed a volatile range of emotions in Ashley. No wonder she felt jittery and disoriented. After countless mental arguments against going with Michael, she kept coming back to one immutable fact. She was irresistibly drawn to him, wanted him in every way, and no longer cared to pretend otherwise.

It was odd how fate sometimes intervened and altered the pattern of a person's life. Before they'd been marooned in the elevator, Michael had seemed too invincible, too able to control everything and everyone around him—most of all, her. The kind of man she didn't dare let too close. True, a few times he'd tempted her, yet no matter how strong his appeal, Ashley had presumed she would eventually pull back.

All that changed with the revelation of his claustrophobia. That sign of vulnerability had been her undoing. It was totally illogical to reverse her decision to limit her dealings with Michael simply to professional ones because of that brief interlude when she had provided Michael with comfort. Yet, once her empathetic impulse had been evoked, she could no longer subdue it.

Ashley realized that theirs was a relationship that could, in all probability, bring her grief and heartbreaking loss. This time, she was willing to risk it.

By leaving the choice up to her, Michael had made Ashley confront her feelings for him and act on them. It was a shrewd gambit. He'd been right to force the issue. They couldn't have gone on much longer with so much unresolved between them.

While packing this morning, Ashley was convinced that she wasn't acting impulsively by taking the trip with Michael.

Now, if she could only stop her heart from pounding. Ashley wanted to approach their weekend with the panache of a woman who'd done this sort of thing often enough to be blasé. But she couldn't; hence her case of jitters. She knew that sometime during the weekend she and Michael would become lovers, and she had to broach the subject before they arrived at the lake. After that, it would be too late.

Michael knocked. She opened the door and continued to clutch the door handle even after he'd entered the room.

"I think you can let go of that," he joked. "I'm in." Ashley attempted a weak smile.

"What's up? Haven't changed your mind, have you?" Michael asked with concern.

"No, it's not that. It's—" She broke off, feeling increasingly embarrassed. "Michael, it's been a long time since I . . . That is, I'm not too, uh, practiced." *Practiced? Great choice of words.*

"You think I'm looking for a sexual gymnast?"

She shook her head. "No. Technique is the least of my worries." That was enough of a lie to turn the chrome door handle slippery beneath her sweaty palm. "It's just that . . . What I mean is—"

"You want me to take care of contraception."

A smile broke through her apprehension, and she directed it at him. "Now, why didn't I think of that? It sounds so simple."

"It is. And it's already taken care of."

"Oh." Her smile slipped a fraction. "I guess you're always prepared for—" Ashley cut off the statement with a laugh. "I'm making you sound like a Boy Scout." In contrast, she sounded like a nervous ninny.

Michael took her other hand. By some miracle it wasn't half as clammy as the one glued to the door. "Ash, we're spending a couple of days together. You

know I want us to make love, but I promise nothing
is going to happen that you're not ready for and comfortable with."

"Don't try to tell me you've gone to all this trouble
to arrange a platonic weekend. I'm not that naive."
She glanced down at her watch, then at Michael's
hand covering hers. It seemed symbolic. Why was she
waffling when her mind was made up? With renewed
courage, she yanked on the handle. "Let's get my suitcase and beat it back to work. We'll have plenty of
time for talk later."

IT WAS AFTER DARK when they arrived at the Jordans'
lake house. They'd shopped for groceries before leaving the city and stopped later for dinner. Ashley had
worried she'd be uptight the whole way there; but
aside from a growing feeling of anticipation, she was
amazingly calm.

She hadn't given much thought to what the lake
house would be like, though she'd hoped it wasn't so
primitive that it lacked running water and electricity.
Trailing Michael as he raised windows to air out the
musty interior, she discovered the house was far from
rustic.

"We'll leave these open a few minutes before I turn
on the heat."

They had entered through a long, narrow kitchen
that was more modern and convenient than the one

in Ashley's Atlanta apartment. The living room, which was enormous, had sliding-glass doors that opened onto a deck.

"I'll put your stuff in Diana's room," Michael said, standing in front of the fieldstone fireplace.

She had assumed they would share. Instead, she followed him into his sister's room, then watched while he carried his duffel bag into a larger room, obviously the master bedroom. Ashley vacillated between relief and disappointment that he intended them to sleep separately.

When they were back in the kitchen, he suggested, "Why don't you unload the food while I flush the antifreeze out of the plumbing?"

"Antifreeze?"

"Minnesota, remember? We have to take our winters seriously. With no heat in the house, if I didn't shut off the water and drain the pipes, we'd be standing in a major mess."

"Of course. I spent four years in Michigan, but I'd forgotten." She shivered, remembering her freshman year when her roommate had given her a survival kit to keep in the car. A lifelong Southerner, Ashley had dismissed the warnings until she heard about a coed freezing to death when her car stalled in a blizzard. At the time, she'd wondered why anyone choose to live in such an inhospitable climate.

Now she was questioning her own choice to be here. Her calm had deserted her, to be replaced by apprehension. Did she have a prayer of pulling this off with any degree of sophistication? Or would she be as inept as she feared? As she unpacked the food, she replayed Kitty's advice to her: *You have the strength to take charge of your life. Make it whatever you wish it to be.*

Once housekeeping tasks were completed, they put on jackets and went on to the deck. Moonlight glimmered through tall trees. It was utterly still except for the occasional cry of a loon.

"Though I'm not much of an outdoor person, I'm beginning to understand why solitude appeals to people," Ashley said in a hushed tone.

Michael's hand rested lightly on her shoulder. "After a few days here, I always feel like I can go home and tackle anything. I was glad when my parents decided not to sell it when they moved away. Now that my dad's semiretired, he comes back often to fish."

Ashley remembered the family picture she had seen on the houseboat—the one that looked as if they'd all been having such fun here. "Does your mother come with him?"

His laugh was harsh. "Not anymore. She's too busy with her career."

This wasn't the first time she'd heard disapproval in connection with his mother's work. "I can't believe you object to a woman having a career."

He braced his forearms on the deck railing. "I don't object to women having careers, as long as they don't get absorbed in them to the exclusion of everything else, especially their families."

"In other words, now that her children have left home, it's okay for your mother to have a job as long as it doesn't interfere with her real job—catering to your father's every whim."

"That's some conclusion you jumped to," he said in a level tone. "And a wrong one."

"You claim I'm wrong. Yet it's clear you resent your mother's career."

"It isn't the career, dammit! It's how it has changed her. She's never at home when we call, and when she does call us back, all we hear about is how busy she is. It's like we're imposing on her. I really worry about my dad. He's miserable."

"Of course. You men have to stick together. It's all her fault, right?" Ashley wondered if she was defending the unknown Mrs. Jordan or herself. Or was she purposely picking a fight to drive a wedge between her and Michael so she could avoid what was really tying her in knots? If that was the case, she'd do better to pick another cause. This one hit too close to home. She couldn't seem to stop herself. "Did either you or your father ever stop to consider that maybe your mother deserves a chance to do what she wants? Why does everyone assume it's a woman's duty to move all over the country because her husband is transferred? When it comes to her career, it's tolerated only if it doesn't inconvenience anyone else."

"Ashley," Michael said quietly, turning to face her again, "we're not talking about the same issues. If I sound resentful, it's because I always thought my parents had something special and precious—something I hoped to be lucky enough to find someday. Now I see it falling apart." One fist pounded his opposite palm. "I hate watching over thirty years of a good, loving marriage go down the tube. Nothing is worth losing that."

How could she dispute that?

"It isn't necessary to start an argument to keep me from jumping you, Ash. I don't really want to discuss my parents' problems. Not tonight."

She knew quite well what was on tonight's agenda. Chastened, Ashley bit her lip and waited for him to make the first move. It didn't take long. Michael turned her around so he could massage her shoulder muscles.

"Ever since we pulled in the driveway, I've watched you getting wound up tighter by the second," he told her.

"I know. I keep talking to myself and taking deep breaths. So far it's not working. I'm sorry."

"Don't apologize." He continued the massage. "Remember what I told you in the car this afternoon? There's no reason to pressure yourself. Turn around and look at me."

She did, slowly. There it was again—that tender, accepting smile that made her long to give Michael everything he wanted, damn the cost. She took another deep gulp of air. "Don't pay any attention to me. I tend to get stressed out in unfamiliar situations. I'll get over it. I'm trying."

"Ashley, listen to me. If you have to psyche yourself up this much so we can go to bed together, it isn't going to turn out all that great for either of us. Let's just drop the idea for now and concentrate on getting you comfortable." He tugged her back inside. "When you've had a hard day at work, or are tense, how do you go about relaxing?"

"Soak in a hot bath. Have a drink sometimes."

"So, go soak in the tub for as long as you want. When you're finished I'll have a warm drink ready. Then you can go to bed, alone, and get a good night's sleep. I have a big day planned tomorrow. We can both use the rest." He pushed her in the direction of his sister's bedroom. "I don't know about you, but last night wasn't one of my better ones."

Ashley resisted the urge to hug him. "Thanks for being so understanding."

"You might say I owe you. I pushed pretty hard to get you here. It's enough for now that you have a good time. So, go take your bath and stop agonizing."

In the guest bathroom, Ashley twisted the taps on full force and berated herself for turning into a shrew. She had jumped up on a soapbox, spouting off about equality of the sexes because she wasn't at ease with her own sexuality. Earlier she'd been quite confident; however, the moment Michael shut off the car engine, she'd been besieged by doubts.

Perhaps he was right. She'd follow his advice and stop fretting. Ashley sank into the hot, foamy water and closed her eyes.

She revived one of her favorite fantasies. She was lying on white, soothingly hot sand on a deserted beach. In Tahiti. The sun beat down on her bare back, lulling her to sleep. Beads of water from the gently lapping breakers, only a few yards from where she lay, formed a fine, cooling mist on her heated body.

The heat was very real. It spread over her breasts, stomach, legs. Between them. Water lapped at her nipples, stimulating and sensitizing them. Michael insinuated himself into her reverie.

She blinked and looked around her. She was alone in the steamy bathroom. She returned to her fantasy. Again, Michael was with her.

Rubbing soap on a washcloth, she asked herself why Michael had this effect on her when no other male had ever reached her on so deep a level. Ashley was quite aware of the reason she always shied away from emotional and physical closeness with any man. It was a matter of being practical. Sex was not a priority. She presumed she'd never marry—after all wasn't she an "Atwood maiden aunt," like Kitty? Consequently it made no sense to get entangled in a relationship that could go nowhere.

But that was exactly what she was about to do—get entangled. She wanted to think the choice had been hers when, in reality, it was as if she'd had no choice. Or was she deceiving herself? Did she really want Michael so badly that she would use any rationalization that allowed her to have him?

Whatever her motivation, she was fed up with trying to analyze it. Michael had made her aware of the sexuality she had suppressed for so long; made her vibrantly aware of being female. No more cowering in the bathroom, no more mixed signals. Tonight, she decided, Michael would have no doubts about her message.

Ashley finished bathing, dried quickly and surveyed the contents of her small suitcase. What had she brought that lent itself to seduction? She had nothing remotely sexy, except her underwear. She could hardly slink in and greet Michael wearing that. At last she settled for white cotton slacks with a drawstring waist, and a rose-colored sweater. After loosening her hair from the twist, she vigorously brushed until it swirled around her shoulders.

When she came back to the living room, a blazing fire crackled in the fireplace. She sank onto one of the low couches flanking the hearth, and gazed at the flames. A lone saxophone's haunting, smoky notes issued from the stereo, heightening the charged sensuality of the room. Michael may have told her to drop the idea of going to bed together, nevertheless, the setting he'd staged appeared like a carefully orchestrated prelude.

"Feel better?" Wearing old, washed-out jeans and a sweatshirt, he came toward her, his soft moccasins scarcely whispering on the wooden floor. He dropped down beside her and placed two glasses on the table in front of them.

"Mmm . . . the bath was very relaxing."

"I was all set for a cold shower. At the last minute I reminded myself I'm no masochist." He sampled his drink, nodded his approval and tipped the glass again. Eyeing her over the rim, he grinned and said, "Probably wouldn't have done much good, anyway."

Ashley smiled and took a sip of her drink. "This is good, too. What is it?"

"A splash of hot water, a dash of sugar, a lemon twist. And Armagnac."

"Ah, the magic ingredient. You have excellent taste."

"Selective." His knuckles rubbed against hers, as they both still held their hands wrapped around their crystal glasses. "My taste in women is especially selective."

Ashley felt his lips graze her temple before he settled back and they weren't touching at all. His heat lingered, though. Lingered and spread. Unspoken mutual desire bound them together. It was so palpable she could feel it. And she wanted more.

She made an almost imperceptible move closer to him—the distance small, the decision behind it significant. Michael recognized the subtle gesture for the invitation it was, and his tongue stole out to taste the fragrance of her neck, at the bend of her elbow, on her inner wrists. "Some nights, in the dark, I've sworn your perfume was all around me. Maybe it was only inside my head."

Ashley trembled. These sensations were so new to her, so provocative. She savored them slowly.

"Do you think about me, Ash? Last thing before you sleep and first thing when you wake?"

"Yes!" she murmured, confessing at last. "Every night. I even dream about you. That first night—" Something stopped her from admitting how erotic her dreams about him had been after she'd known him only a matter of hours.

"Me, too. I woke up in bad shape." With his hand pressed against the fly of his jeans, his gaze met hers. "I started wanting you that morning in your hotel lobby, and the ache hasn't let up since. I'm beginning to think it never will."

"It will," she breathed, tunneling her hand beneath his, curving her fingers to mold the shape of him. "Trust me, I can take care of the ache."

"God, Ashley! What are you trying to do to me, woman?"

"Show you how *much* of a woman I am," she said, confident now that she could convince them both. "Prove I can give you everything you need."

He pulled her tightly to him. "There's nothing to prove. You *are* everything I need."

His words confirmed her own need. She welcomed his tongue, eager for the refined torture of his sustained, lazy stroking.

"Remember what I said about being obsessed by your mouth?"

Nodding, she claimed his tongue again, unwilling to give up a single second of pleasure, especially now that she knew her kiss inflamed him and made him desire her as much as she did him.

"The obsession goes deeper," Michael rasped.

"Deeper?"

"So deep I want to feel it on every inch of me, all of me. Everywhere. And then I want to be inside you."

His words were so powerfully evocative that she could almost feel him fill her. Ashley ached for pleasurable release. "That's what I want, too." She offered him a seductive invitation. "Where shall I start?"

"Right here," he said, standing and pulling her up with him. "Kiss me."

Her hands framed his face as she offered him her mouth, putting everything she had into the kiss. Lips, tongue, teeth—brushes, licks, bites. "Like that?"

"Yeah. I like *that*. Ash, I hope you're ready. I'm going to hold you." His strong arms bound her tightly to him. "Taste you." His tongue flitted along the outline of her lips before plunging inside. "Love you." Every kiss, every stroking caress drove them a step backward until they were pressed against the wall. They meshed perfectly. Michael rotated his hips tantalizingly against Ashley as she impatiently matched his motions.

"I want you," she murmured. "All night."

He flattened both hands on the wall and pushed himself away, groaning. "Honey, talk like that, and the levee's gonna break."

She drew him back to her and sinuously swayed against his heated body. "That's the idea, isn't it?"

"Not yet, it isn't." He took her mouth again, stealing her breath. Sweet hunger and savage need—she experienced both. The word *love* hovered unspoken on her lips.

"Mi-chael?"

His gaze locked with hers. Then he nodded and mouthed the single word "Yes." The passion burning in his eyes was unmistakable.

His lips traced the skin at the neckline of her sweater. His tongue lingered on the slight depression in each shoulder before he drew her sweater over her head and tossed it aside. She was wearing nothing under her sweater. For a long moment, he simply looked.

Ashley's clamorous heartbeat was the only sound in her ears. Her gaze was fixed on the dark depths of his eyes.

"Beautiful," he said at last, bending to encircle each nipple with ethereal kisses.

Feeling the warmth of his breath, the lightness of his touch, was like being driven languorously mad. Ashley grazed his earlobes, his lips, with her fingertips; then ran them down his chest. She pushed up his sweatshirt, eager to meld the softness of her breasts with the rougher texture of his chest. The contrast was unbearably exciting. She couldn't get her fill of touching him. Her hands gently massaged his shoulders and his arms, then circled around to his back.

He tore off the sweatshirt and stilled her hands when he captured her mouth in a kiss that pushed all thought from her mind. As his lips traveled steadily downward, he knelt and skimmed the slacks over her hips and down her legs. They landed on the sweater.

His hands were everywhere, curious, thorough, insatiable. *We're not even going to make it out of the living room.*

Michael then took her hand and led her through the door into the master bedroom.

He brought her fingers to the top metal button of his jeans, then guided them down to free each one. Ashley had never realized how sexy button-fly jeans were, how alluring the act of opening them, one by one, could be.

Their remaining clothes disappeared on the way across the room, and they fell to the bed, facing each other.

"Hold on to me," he rasped. "Hold on."

Placing her hands on his shoulders, he slid down so that the tip of his tongue could flick over her breasts, dampening and teasing her soft, yielding flesh.

She watched while he made her wet, writhing helplessly when the wanton excitement became too much to bear. This time she guided her nipple to his mouth and asked him for what she needed. Michael's groan, followed by his greedy suction told Ashley he found her newfound boldness as exciting as she did.

"Don't make me wait. I can't . . . stand it," Ashley whispered. Instinctively, her hips lifted in a silent plea for him to enter her.

Michael inhaled deeply and inched away. "Honey, slow down a little. We don't have to rush. Especially our first time."

"The first time, especially, I want to rush. I'm tired of anticipating." Eager with desire, she rubbed against his fingers, "And I'm ready."

No more ready than he was, Michael thought, barely hanging on to his control. Maybe she was right. They'd waited long enough. He could handle "slow and easy" better when he wasn't aroused to the point of being explosive.

He reached into the nightstand drawer for a little foil packet.

"Do you want to make love, Ashley? Now?"

Eyes wide, she nodded. "Then help me," he said.

As she covered his erection with the protective sheath, he groaned with anticipation. Neither moved for a few seconds until Ashley pulled him to her. "Now, Michael."

"Yes. Now." With a long, slow, fluid thrust he made them one. "Oh, Ashley," he murmured against her ear. "Ashley."

She held him tighter, anxious for the long-awaited release. As Michael responded with slow, controlled strokes, Ashley moved in rhythm with him. When he slipped his palms under her hips to intensify her pleasure, she sank her fingers into his shoulders.

She gave herself to him totally, completely, until the rush of pulsating ecstasy overwhelmed them.

"Michael!" Her cry blended with the muted sound of his release, uniting them in passionate communion.

7

AT THE SOUND OF running water, Ashley stirred, battling the fuzziness inside her head. There shouldn't be anyone in her room. She always woke alone. When she heard someone approaching the bed, she struggled up on one elbow and squinted.

Michael. Naked. She flopped back down, and pulled the blanket over herself.

"Come on, lazybones. I know you're in there."

Then he stretched out beside her. By the time he had her tucked snugly against him she was fully awake.

"I don't remember dropping off, or even being sleepy," she mumbled. "I must have been really tired out." She yawned for emphasis.

"Worn-out, are you? I am, too." Burrowing under the sheet, he hugged her. "You were only out for a few minutes. It's just past midnight." One of his legs worked between hers; his fingers spanned her stomach and flexed. "Need a snack?"

"What kind of snack?" Her voice was husky.

"Depends—" he bent over and gave his attention to her ear "—on what you're hungry for."

Ashley shifted restlessly, needing him closer. Her hunger for him was even stronger than before—another thing she hadn't planned on. Had she actually thought making love with him once would be enough?

Michael inspired thoughts so lustful they shocked her. Nothing had prepared her for the sharing of something more profound than the gratification of physical needs. She no longer wanted to hold back. Which added another dimension to her already complicated feelings. This, however, wasn't the time for reflection—not when his mouth was pressed so insistently against her and she could feel him hard against her hip. She ran both hands up and down the smooth musculature of his back. "Your lips are so soft."

"Not as soft as you are, all over. Like here—" he stroked her breasts with his hands "—and here—" he moved his hand down to rub her stomach "—and here—" he rested his palms on her inner thighs. One finger slipped between her legs. He turned to kiss her.

"You kiss like—"

"Like I have my mouth on the most desirable woman I've ever known? Like I can't get enough of her?"

He moved lower, scattering warm, wet promises along her ribs, around her waist, across her stomach. "Because you are. And I can't."

He synchronized the luxuriant probing of his tongue around her navel with the electrifying glide of his finger. Ashley whimpered, knowing she couldn't withstand the deliciousness much longer.

"Michael, please. Come to me."

"In a minute," he said against her quivering stomach. "But first . . ." Intensifying the rhythm and pace of his stroking, he brought her to a shattering climax, then enveloped her in a close, loving embrace. Feather-light passes of his hands over her damp skin soothed her.

Ashley lay still, reeling from the tumultuous release she'd just experienced. Her eyes burned, though she had no idea what had provoked the unshed tears. She didn't feel like crying, yet hot drops were wetting her lashes, trickling out against her will. When Michael rained soft kisses on her forehead and eyelids she averted her face, pressing it to his chest.

"Ashley? You okay, honey?"

She wasn't sure, but gave a vigorous nod to reassure him. She loved his gentleness and concern, so at odds with the urgency he must be feeling. Rigid against her thigh was the evidence that he'd devoted himself to her pleasure while denying his own. A condition she *wanted* to remedy. Reaching between them, she said, "Michael, you didn't . . . Let me . . ."

He was on top of her, poised to enter before she could wrap her fingers around him. "I will. With you."

He buried himself deeply and, pumping hard, fast, found his satisfaction in her depths.

Hearing his prolonged, primal moan echoing in her ear, Ashley came again, violently and unexpectedly.

It seemed like an eternity before she could speak. "Are there earthquakes in this part of Minnesota?"

He chuckled weakly. "Only on the third weekend of May in odd-numbered years." His breath hit her shoulder, harsh and hot. "Lord, I don't think I can move." He tried, but ended up collapsing back on her. "Ashley Atwood, you are one hell of a woman."

A short time later, Ashley drifted into sleep, smiling. She had two more days to glory in the image Michael had of her.

SHE MUST HAVE BEEN asleep for only a few hours when the rattle of dishes next to her head roused her. Ashley opened her eyes to discover a fully dressed Michael, carrying a tray. It took a Herculean effort to sit up and wind the sheet around herself, sari-fashion.

"Figured you'd like breakfast in bed," he said, arranging the tray on her lap.

What she'd like was a lot more sleep, but since he'd brought tea, fruit and croissants, she might reconsider. "What time is it?" When he told her it was ten after six, she nearly choked on the tea. "I prefer to sleep in on my days off. You're going to be in trouble, unless you have a good reason for getting me up so early."

"The best. It's walleye season and we're going to catch our limit. I told you we'd have some fun."

"Fishing?"

"Of course. Isn't that why you came up here?" he asked with a deadpan expression on his face.

"Of course." So she was to be subjected to another of Michael's outdoor excursions. She'd survived several already. The problem today was how she could come off as a good sport without having to put a worm on a hook. It wouldn't be easy, but she'd go to any lengths to avoid handling live bait. "When does this adventure begin?"

"Not for a while yet. I'll give you the rest of the tour, and then get the boat out. After a long winter, it takes a while to convince the motor to start. Like all old-timers, it's kind of crotchety." He poured her some more tea and, after she polished off the remaining food, lifted the tray and left Ashley alone to get ready.

She took a quick shower which left her warmer and wide-awake, but still unenthusiastic about fishing. Wrapped in a towel, she came back to the bedroom and found a department-store bag on the bed. Inside were a new pair of jeans and a red sweatshirt with the message Minnesota Swat Team stenciled across the front. She laughed at the sketch of cartoon figures chasing gigantic mosquitoes with flyswatters below the lettering. Both items of clothing were the correct size. He must have been sure she'd come with him. Since inviting her Thursday night, there had been no time when he could have gone shopping. She dressed and went in search of Michael.

Good sport, Ashley reminded herself, breezing into the living room. "Thanks for the jeans," she said to Michael.

"I guessed at the size," he told her, his eyes gleaming with approval. "Ready?"

Ashley nodded and trailed him out the sliding-glass door, wishing everything he said didn't evoke sensual images. A single night in his arms had transformed her into a wanton—a feat she'd assumed impossible.

Outside she saw details of the exterior she'd missed last night in the dark. One end of the deck had been screened-in to create a porch off the dining area. Michael gestured toward it and then touched one of the insects imprinted on the front of her shirt. "These critters are vicious on summer nights. A screened-in porch cuts down on the bloodletting."

At the opposite end of the deck was a grill and picnic space. From there, a breezeway connected the house to a guest suite. He pointed out a large dorm-like room over the garage where he, his brother and their visiting friends used to sleep. "That kept us obnoxious teenage boys away from everyone else."

Interpreting her open mouth as an invitation, he leaned close to kiss her. Ashley delighted in the almost instant reaction of his body, and pushed her hands under his sweatshirt to bring him closer. They swayed, lost in a sea of tactile sensations until she drew back and teased, "Is this some new kind of fishing I don't know about?"

Michael stared at her mouth a few seconds before breaking into a grin and shaking his head. "There isn't much that would distract me from the walleye opener, but you've given me a better idea."

"Now, now," she reprimanded, shaking her finger. "You promised me fishing, and I'm panting to see what all the excitement is about."

"Okay, you win. Fishing first." He gave her a look hot enough to melt the rubber soles of her shoes. "Panting and excitement later."

Ashley used her smile to signal to him a clear message: *I can't wait.* If she wasn't careful, she could really get into this business of being "one hell of a woman."

When Michael raised the garage door, Ashley giggled at the two-toned pink-and-white boat with exaggerated rear fins. "I should have guessed you'd have a boat that looks like a '57 Plymouth."

"You're laughing at a genuine antique," he complained with injured pride. "I would have thought that you of all people would appreciate this treasure." He vaulted into an equally aged jeep and ground away until it started.

Within a few minutes, he had hooked onto the trailer and launched the boat. They stowed poles and tackle, and while he coaxed the boat's motor to life, she went back to the house to collect some warm jackets and snacks.

The lake was frigid, although it was well into May. As the boat skipped along the water's surface, swells of icy spray slapped Ashley's face. She pulled her hood forward around her head, blessing Michael's mother for leaving behind a down jacket and lined gloves. How come Michael was so impervious to the cold, while she, bundled in the quilted parka, was blue with chill?

After about fifteen minutes Michael shut off the motor, and as they drifted he pulled out a slimy worm and worked it onto a hook. Repulsed, Ashley shuddered, keeping her mouth shut.

"Don't sweat it. I'll bait your hook and remove your fish—this time. Next trip, it's your job."

She could have informed him that there'd be no next time. She didn't want to think about that grim inevitability—much less discuss it. "What is that thing?" She indicated the slimy blackish lump he was threading onto a second hook.

"Leech." She shuddered again and his lips twitched. "When it's your turn, I'll get night crawlers or minnows."

"Great. I always considered night crawlers the bait of choice." He laughed and handed her the rod. "What do I do now?" she asked.

He started another small motor that purred almost noiselessly. "We're going to troll." At Ashley's blank look, he explained, "Move along slowly and wait for a bite. When you feel a strike, give it a little play, then set the hook and reel it in nice and easy." He demonstrated the technique and Ashley told him it sounded like a snap.

"We'll soon find out, won't we?"

They fished for several hours; sometimes in companionable silence, sometimes trading opinions about everything from government to Woody Allen movies. They agreed that the former was a hopeless morass, while the latter made a lot of sense. At frequent intervals during their conversation, Ashley was struck by the notion that this was how normal people carried on courtships, and fell in love. When that idea popped into her head, she quickly suppressed it and concentrated on snagging another fish.

By eleven o'clock, she'd caught her allotted six, due more to beginner's luck than skill. "Shall I help you with your limit?" she volunteered sweetly, pointing to Michael's one walleye.

"You know what we do with braggarts, don't you?"
Without waiting for an answer, he went on. "First we
toss 'em overboard and make them swim to shore.
Then they have to clean everyone's catch."

"In that case, please accept my sincere apology. I felt
that water temperature and I've no desire to become
a blue Popsicle."

"Plus something tells me that if I want these fish for
dinner, I'd better not turn you loose on them with a
knife." Michael shut off the trolling motor and started
the outboard. "Guess you lucked out again."

He steered a course for their wharf and, when they
docked, sent her to the house. Ashley didn't argue.
She didn't want any part of butchering those poor
fish.

Since it was almost noon, she raided the refrigerator. Even if she wasn't the world's greatest cook, she
could throw something together that would pass for
lunch. Humming, she emptied a container of frozen
soup into a covered casserole dish and shoved it into
the microwave. Last night at the store when she said
she'd never tasted wild-rice soup, Michael had tossed
it into their cart, announcing it was a Minnesota spe-
cialty that she had to try.

He had introduced her to a number of Minnesota
specialties during the three weeks since her arrival.
Only one really counted, though—the man himself.

Being with him had opened Ashley's eyes in more ways than one.

While still proclaiming her lack of interest in exercise and outdoor activities, she secretly had enjoyed the picnic, hikes and bike riding. Even the fishing hadn't been as bad as she'd expected. She supposed it was the novelty that intrigued her. Maybe it was her companion who made the difference. Ashley knew no one else could have convinced her to attempt half as much as Michael had. Certainly no man had ever tempted her into bed with the facility Michael had.

She grabbed up a chef's knife and attacked a wedge of cheese. Her finger narrowly escaped a vicious swipe of the blade. She took a deep breath and tried again. It would help if she pictured herself as a woman of the world who could carry on a short-term affair with aplomb. That wasn't the real Ashley Atwood—the one who guarded her body as protectively as she did her emotions. Yet what was she to make of the fact that Michael had unmasked her with such ease?

For years she'd been so unapproachable that few men bothered to ask her out. Starting from the moment they met, Michael simply overrode all her objections. Why had she opened up to this particular man?

One man. That was the sum total of her prior experience. After what she'd shared with Michael, Ashley realized that experience hardly counted. She couldn't blame the fellow graduate student she'd selected to initiate her. He'd been bright, willing and genuinely nice. It was her own motivation that had been all wrong.

Curiosity, not desire, had prompted her to experiment. She had wanted to experience the mystique of sex. Her mouth tightened in disgust. No wonder she'd come away asking, "Is that all there is?"

Michael had shown her just how much there was, and that was more than likely going to haunt her. She had never missed physical intimacy because she'd never known it. What would her life be like, now that she had?

Maybe Scarlett O'Hara had had the right idea: Think about unpleasant things tomorrow. Telling herself she had tomorrow to seek answers and only days to spend with Michael, she slapped cheese, tomatoes and lettuce on thick slices of mayo-slathered bread. She loaded the sandwiches, bowls of soup and a basket of fruit onto the tray Michael had used for breakfast. The sun was high overhead, and warm enough that she'd exchanged her heavier clothes for a T-shirt and camp shorts. Eating outside would be pleasant.

Her timing was faultless. Michael stepped onto the deck with a pan of cleaned fish soaking in water as she deposited the tray on the round redwood table. "Give me a minute to put these in the fridge and soap off the smell. Be right back."

Ashley sat on a bench and put out their spoons and napkins. For some reason she envisioned her sister arranging silver on her eighteenth-century mahogany dining table. The thought brought a smile. She could also imagine Cooper's opinion of Ashley spending a secluded weekend with a man she had met only weeks ago.

"Does that smile mean something I ought to know about?"

"Only if you're into sterling and mahogany."

Michael dropped onto the bench at right angles to hers, his gaze sliding leisurely over every part of her. "At the moment, I'm into other things."

Like everything else about Michael, his voice was vibrant and seductive. Before meeting him, Ashley hadn't imagined that desire could be an almost constant state. From the way he looked at her, she realized it was the same for him. She took a hefty bite of her sandwich, unwilling to face how long it might take her to recover from this extraordinary time with Michael.

"Thanks for fixing lunch," he said, spooning up soup.

She gestured at their meal. "You are looking at the entire range of my talent in the kitchen. Opening soup containers and building sandwiches is about the peak of my culinary skill, I'm afraid."

"Then it's a good thing you've got me here. Tonight I'll show off what I can do with our catch."

They finished eating, joking and teasing each other about their morning outing. It was as if the two of them had done this many times before.

"You know," Michael said, pulling the fruit bowl toward him, "I like you this way—not hidden beneath layers of starch and suits."

Ashley tensed. "This isn't the first time you've made comments like that. What's wrong with my wearing suits to work? That's the way professionals should dress."

He looked out over the lake instead of at her. "Right. Especially if they want to disguise the fact that they're also women."

"What has that got to do with being a woman? You didn't seem to have any complaints last night." His head jerked around and Ashley could have bitten her tongue. Defensiveness had sparked those rash words.

"Last night," he pointed out with a lazy smile, "you weren't wearing *anything* to hide beneath. I thought I made it clear how much I like the other you."

"There is no *other* me," she snapped. "Don't make the mistake of thinking you can turn me into something I'm not." She began putting their dishes and utensils in precise stacks on the tray.

"You're arranging those exactly like you do your papers," Michael observed with a nod at her hands. "Trying to conjure up the accountant, Ash?"

"Why not?" she returned flippantly. "That's what I am, and I won't apologize, because I don't need to be anything else."

He scoffed. "So a career is enough for you? You don't need something more?"

Ashley's fingers gripped the spoons tightly. How had the ease they'd shared a few minutes ago degenerated so fast? "I suppose you mean a husband and children. No, I don't need that." She said each word quite distinctly and wondered why she found them almost painful. "It's a myth that women can have it all."

Michael lifted her hand and brushed his lips over her fingers. "The world is full of myths, Ash. It's up to you to pick which ones you believe."

She didn't care to decipher his cryptic advice, nor could she bear for this disagreement to ruin the mood of their weekend. They had too little time left to waste it arguing about something neither of them could alter. She changed the subject and went back to tidying up the table. "You sit still while I take care of these dishes. What's in store for me this afternoon?"

"How about a walk in the woods? Maybe the wild violets are blooming."

"Not me," Ashley stated, shaking her head. "These aren't like those city woods close to your condo. These are the genuine article. Lots of beasties with multiple legs and stingers and Bunyanesque appetites. No, thanks."

"You're just protesting out of habit. You know you'll get a kick out of it once you try it. Come on. Leave the dishes."

Michael got a camera from the back seat of Agnes and directed her toward the dense woods that bounded the Jordan property on two sides.

Ashley balked before stepping out of the clearing, grabbing hold of a birch sapling to halt their advance. "I guarantee there's a nice fertile patch of poison ivy with my name on it. What are you going to do about that?"

"Why, protect you from it, naturally." He looped his arm around her shoulder and grinned down at her. "Barring that, I'll find the calamine lotion . . . and rub it all over you. Real slow."

BEFORE THEY WENT TO SLEEP that night, Michael had delivered on every one of his promises. With their walleye, he proved himself an accomplished cook. From there, they moved on to taking a lengthy shower together that had little to do with getting clean and a lot to do with extended foreplay.

Though he'd protected her from poison ivy, he rubbed not calamine, but a luscious-smelling lotion all over her. Real slow. The lovemaking that followed was boundless and satiating.

8

DELECTABLE SMELLS tempted Ashley to open her eyes. Good heavens! Almost eleven. Even when she meant to be a sluggard, she seldom slept until ten. Of course she could use the excuse of having stayed up very late last night. And Michael had again woken her at six this morning. She stretched languidly, her smile turning dreamy. Today he hadn't had fishing on his mind.

Now she could hear him banging around in the kitchen, making a huge mess, no doubt. He cooked with great zest, and the aftermath resembled a war zone. But you couldn't argue with success. Dinner had been scrumptious. How often she had heard her friends lament, "Oh, for a man who can cook!"

Of course, Michael had a lot more going for him than expertise in the kitchen. He was intelligent, fun, good-looking and talented. And a wonderfully imaginative lover—sometimes tender, sometimes wild—but never less than devastating.

She sat up, dangling her legs over the edge of the rumpled bed. A hundred tiny aches attested to how thoroughly involved she'd been as Michael's partner in lovemaking.

Lovemaking. Ashley had always considered the word an amusing euphemism. So many people looked upon sex as a guilty pleasure, one that required a lofty term to justify it. After having spent two nights in Michael's arms, she understood that what they'd shared was infinitely more complicated than having sex. It *was* making love.

That word sent her sprinting to the shower. *Don't be a dope*, she lectured herself, letting the water beat down on her back. *You aren't falling in love and neither is he. Can't happen. Too messy, too difficult. Impossible.*

Lathering herself with vigorous swipes of the soap, she continued the reprimand. *Lust. An acute case of lust. That's what I'm suffering from.* It had to be. If she allowed her thoughts to stray beyond that, she'd be setting herself up for a monumental fall.

She dried her hair and dressed in the slacks she'd worn so briefly on Friday night. She'd have preferred to wear something else, but her choices were limited. She only hoped that every time she put them on in the future, she wasn't reminded of Michael taking them off, and all that had followed. *Enough, already!* If that happened, she'd throw away the damned pants.

"Good," Michael said when she wandered into the dining area. "You're ready. How about setting the table while I dish this up?"

She did as he asked, then sat at the place she'd occupied last night. He looked so capable and so damned lovable that she wanted to wrap herself around him and stay that way forever.

He deposited the plate before her with a flourish. "Eggs Hussarde."

"Like at Brennan's?"

"Straight out of their cookbook."

She sampled the hollandaise-topped eggs and found them as tasty as those she'd eaten in New Orleans. "Well, you've done it again. You're spoiling me with all these terrific meals. How am I supposed to go back to a routine of mediocre hotel and restaurant food?"

She intended her remark to sound light and cheerful. His answer was serious and wistful. "If that's all it would take to keep you here, I think I'd be willing to cook forever."

Ashley's eyes flickered closed, then rose to meet his. That one statement changed everything. No longer were they talking about a casual weekend together. Michael was clearly indicating that he wanted a future, after she'd told him from the start that it wasn't an option for them. It was risky to let him get close. She had spent too much time with him, gotten to know him too well—foolishly ignoring common sense.

He reached across and soothingly stroked her arm. "Stop looking trapped, Ash. I won't push for anything you can't give."

Didn't he understand? A man like Michael deserved so much, and there was nothing she could give.

It was apparent now that they both would be hurt by her selfishness.

Footsteps slapping across the deck interrupted her depressing thought. Michael scrambled to his feet.

"Doug!"

"Well, well, big brother. I tried to get in touch with you every night last week about coming up for walleye opener." His brows arched eloquently. "But I see you had other fish to fry."

Michael's younger brother—Ashley recognized him from the family pictures displayed in the houseboat.

He strode past Michael, homing in on Ashley with the innate skill of a man assured of his effect on the opposite sex. Smiling at his target, he asked, "And who have we here?"

Michael assessed his brother a long time before speaking. "Ashley Atwood, my brother, Doug."

Surprised at the terse introduction, she smiled and extended her hand. "I'm glad to meet you." Ashley assessed him. Though he was taller and brawnier than Michael, he hadn't a spark of Michael's magnetism.

"My pleasure," he assured her. "I love your accent."

"Listen, bud," Michael interrupted in a firm voice. "This one is strictly off-limits. Not negotiable." He stepped toward the taller man and rapped Doug's chest with an index finger. "Don't even consider it."

Ashley glanced from one brother to the other. Doug's eyes twinkled with laughter; Michael's expression was enigmatic. His arms were crossed, his bare feet planted in an aggressive stance. Surely this was some form of fraternal horseplay?

"What's going on?" she demanded. "Are you threatening Doug?"

Doug chuckled and slouched into the chair Michael had been using. "I love it. Mikey's acting territorial." He leaned closer to Ashley and lowered his voice. "See, since we were teenagers, I've been known to steal a few of his girlfriends." He shook his head as with mock puzzlement. "He never *used* to act testy about it. Getting possessive in your old age?"

Rubbing the back of his neck, Michael replied sharply. "We get the picture, Doug. Now leave it alone. Remember, I can still put out your lights with one hand."

Michael grinned at his brother. Ashley wasn't too sure if he was joking or not.

Lifting his hands in surrender, Doug backed off. "Okay, okay. You know me. A pacifist at heart." His head dipped toward the kitchen. "Do I smell eggs Hussarde?"

Michael's belligerence disappeared. "I'll fix you something. Do you want coffee in the meantime?"

"Sure, but I'll get it." Doug winked at Ashley before following Michael.

While Doug downed two helpings, he and his brother traded family news. Both were pleased that their father would arrive within the next couple of days for a week of fishing. When Doug finished, Michael asked if Ashley would take on cleanup duty so he could show his brother something on the boat. She agreed, hoping that the friction between the two had totally dissipated.

When she'd made order out of the chaos, she found her mystery story and took it out onto the deck. She reclined on a chaise lounge. Since every couple of pages, the private eye got deposed by visions of Michael, she gave up her attempt to read. Her eyes drifted shut. Michael was there, dominating her thoughts and . . . her heart. Would he always? Would that be enough?

Suspended in a drowsy state between sleep and wakefulness, she was roused by soft lips brushing against her mouth. She parted hers and welcomed the real Michael. Not until his kiss became deeper, more insistent, did she open her eyes.

"Hey," she said sleepily.

"Hi, yourself. Awake yet?"

"Uh-hmm. I think so."

"What would you think if I did this?" With the tip of his tongue he drew enticing patterns on the palms of her hands, punctuating them here and there with suggestive little stabs and licks.

"I'd think I was waking up," she responded in a husky voice.

"How about this?" His mouth strayed up her arm and around her throat.

"Definitely awake." Ashley's hands curved around his firm biceps, sighing with pleasure.

His lips nuzzled the valley between her breasts. "Definitely awake is how I need you for what I have in mind."

Stirring against him Ashley drew back, remembering that Doug was in the house. "Where's Doug?"

Michael looked her straight in the eye and said evenly, "He had to take care of something back in the city."

"Michael, what did you do to him?"

"Nothing violent, if that's what you're hinting. We had a man-to-man and I explained the facts to him. Don't worry about Doug, Ash. He's a sharp guy. He catches on fast."

"You *were* kidding when you threatened him, weren't you?"

Michael wrinkled his forehead, as if giving her question serious consideration. "For a few seconds I think I meant it. Doug wasn't kidding about stealing several of my girlfriends in high school. It didn't matter then. It does now. I wanted to make sure he got the message."

"Since he's gone, I guess he got the message. Do you lapse into macho intimidation very often?"

Michael rose from the chaise and stood against the deck railing. "You may not believe this, but I can't remember ever acting like that. I'm as surprised as you." His eyes, warm brown in the sunlight, locked with hers. "I've never regarded myself as the jealous type."

"You were jealous? Of your brother? And me?"

"Eaten up with it."

This was so bizarre. Didn't Michael know she wasn't the kind of woman that inspired displays of masculine jealousy and possessiveness? The jolt of excitement that shot up her spine appalled her.

He advanced toward Ashley, who was now standing beside him. "Let's stop kidding ourselves, Ashley. We're not involved in a casual relationship here."

She backed away from him. Maybe she shouldn't have brought up the incident with Doug. "Of course not. I'm not interested in a relationship, and you—"

"Aren't interested in hearing how much you don't need a man." His hands gripped her shoulders, halting her retreat. "In fact, sweetheart, all I am interested in hearing for the next couple of hours is how you need *me.*"

"Michael, please don't do this. Don't ruin everything."

His hands strayed from her shoulders to her face. He said softly, "Ashley, I . . . There are things I'd like to say to you that I know you're not ready to hear. I want to tell you exactly how I feel about you and what this weekend means to me. But rather than bring us closer, I have a feeling it'd send you running so fast I'd never catch up." He dropped a light kiss on her forehead. "Do you understand what I'm saying?"

She shut her eyes and nodded. He wanted more than a weekend fling. Much more. Her rational side advised her to run; her impulsive side desperately wanted to blurt out that she loved him. She was in love with Michael—and scared to death.

"I can't express it in words—you're too afraid to hear them—so I'll say it in the only way you'll allow me, for now. Open your eyes, Ashley." He looked into her gray eyes. "Will you let me show you? Will you come to bed with me now?"

"Yes," she whispered, because she could refuse him nothing. "Yes."

LATE SUNDAY AFTERNOON, Michael dropped her off at her hotel. He left her feeling more bewildered than ever as a result of their weekend together.

Greatly in need of counsel, Ashley dialed Kitty at five-minute intervals for an hour, and then finally gave up in frustration. She vowed to call her aunt's office the next day if she couldn't reach her later that evening.

To work off her restless energy, she decided to do laps in the hotel pool. Luckily the pool was nearly deserted—probably because it was dinnertime.

Ten laps should do the trick. Years ago, she had been a good swimmer; recently she hadn't had the time to swim regularly. She dived into the pool. Her arms felt rubbery and she was gasping for air after just two laps. Michael was right: she was out of shape. Still, she persisted. When she reached the end of the pool, she did an underwater flip and started another lap.

Finally, when her lungs and limbs couldn't take any more, she dragged herself out of the water. Burying her face in a towel she collapsed onto a lounger. Only when she'd recovered her breath did she spot Mark in a nearby chair. "I didn't expect you and Jack back from Ames until later." Her two co-workers had driven to Iowa State to take in a concert and visit Jack's college roommate. "How long have you been here?"

"About six laps' worth, I think," Mark replied.

"Why didn't you say something?"

He lifted a shoulder. "You looked as if you needed the exertion."

Mark was the only person who knew she'd gone away with Michael. "Soul-searching time, I'm afraid," she admitted.

"Want to talk about it? Lord knows, you've listened to me often enough in the past year. I'd like to return the favor."

Ashley pulled a cover-up over her head. During the punishing workout, she'd concluded her only salvation would be to submerge herself in work and hope she could hold Michael at bay until the audit was finished. "The swim was a good therapy session. I think I've got everything mapped out in my mind."

Mark chuckled. "I hate to burst your bubble, but strategy planned in the head has a way of blowing up on the battlefield."

"Don't I know it." Her weak smile reflected how little confidence she had in her battle plan. Michael had been quiet and pensive on the trip back. Nevertheless, she doubted he was ready to play docile lapdog and let her end their relationship. "But I have to try."

"He's really got you on the rack, doesn't he?" Mark noted accurately. "I'd guess we're talking serious stuff here."

"I'm in so far over my head it's a wonder I haven't drowned already," she said with a hollow laugh. "Good thing we'll be gone in less than two weeks."

Mark leaned forward, elbows on his knees, staring at the azure water. "You're just going to skip town? Leave behind a guy you're head-over-heels crazy about?"

"I have to," she whispered. When Ashley's bottom lip quivered, she bit it. Tears wouldn't provide her with any answers to her dilemma. "I have to."

"I don't see why." Mark turned to face her. "Ashley, in the past twelve months I've learned more than I ever wanted to know about loneliness. At least twice a day I say, 'I'm outta here, on my way to Australia to shake some sense into a certain redhead afflicted with wanderlust.' I'm still not sure I won't do it someday soon."

"But you and Genie are different. You were in love for months before she took off. You lived together, were practically engaged."

"Right, but lonely is lonely. And it's a lousy way to spend your life. Ever been bone-deep lonely, Ashley?"

"Not until tonight," she conceded. Michael had been gone little less than an hour and she ached with the need to see him, touch him.

Mark stood and turned toward the door. "Then the one thing you have to consider is whether you're willing to live in misery."

"I have no choice."

"That's a lie. There are always choices. We all have to reach that conclusion for ourselves." He stuck out his hand. "Come on, I'll buy us some beers to cry in."

UTTERING A CURSE, Michael tossed a tiny northern pike back into the lake. A week ago, he'd fished here with Ashley. More than once, Michael had wished he'd just kept her here in bed, and to hell with everything else.

For the previous five days, Ashley had burrowed herself in work. Not once did he catch her alone. She had stuck to Mark or Jack like flypaper. When she was in her hotel room, she didn't answer the phone. Ashley appeared to be in full retreat. He swore again.

"Want to talk about it, son?" Daniel Jordan picked a small bit of flotsam from his hook, then expertly cast the line to a spot where he'd already caught several impressive walleyes.

Michael grunted and dropped his pole into the bottom of the boat. Why bother to fish when all he could do was miss strikes or reel in sardines? "Talk about what?"

"Whatever's got you so strung out?"

Michael cringed at the description of his condition. Count on his father to cut right to the heart of things. To be honest, he could do with some straight talk. His father, better than anybody, would understand his confusion. "I've met someone." He squinted at the horizon. "Fell real hard, real fast.

"I brought her up here last weekend." The memory filled him with emotion. "For those two days we were . . . good, very good, together. I never knew it could be like that."

Dan made another skillful cast. "I know for a fact you've never brought another woman up here. Guess it must be serious."

"I love her," Michael confessed. He just didn't know what he was going to do about it. "That's where it starts getting sticky."

"When you thought it would be simple?" Dan speculated. "What's the problem?"

"She's an accountant, a traveling workaholic." His mouth hardened. "Worst of all, she insists she doesn't need anything else." He switched his gaze to his father's interested one. "Remind you of anyone?"

Dan reeled in his line and turned toward his son. "I guess you're seeing some similarities between her and your mother."

"Some!" Michael jeered. "They both act like they're on a divine crusade to prove it's possible to chase a career twenty-four hours a day."

"Maybe she got in the habit of spending so much time on her job because she had nothing else. Now that you two are in love, she'll have something—someone—else to pay attention to."

Michael shook his head, recalling the obscene amount of time Ashley had spent at the office last week. Judging from her increasingly haggard appearance, he wondered if she ever left at all. She wouldn't listen when he tried to talk to her about it. She set her shoulders and worked more diligently. He knew she was trying to shut him out, but something else was driving her, too. He'd been careful not to pressure her. Still, she'd worked as if a demon were dogging her heels.

"There are a couple of fallacies in your reasoning, Dad. First, I'm the one in love. I've no idea how she feels—not really. I'm sure she cares about me. Maybe a lot. But she's made it clear that when the audit's finished here, so is she."

"I see the problem. Got a plan for changing her mind?"

"You mean short of chaining her to my bed?" He smiled when Dan rolled his eyes. "Well, satisfactory or not, that's the only solution I keep coming up with. So what's your advice? You've been in the same bind with Mom. Still are."

"We're talking about some major differences here, son. Number one, and most important, is that no matter how busy your mother is, I've never doubted she loves me. You make it sound like your mother never stops working, which isn't quite the case."

"Then how come every time I call she's either out entertaining a client or courting a new one? And she never comes back here with you anymore, never goes anywhere unless it's on business." Michael was shocked at how petulant his condemnation sounded.

"I don't deny she's out a couple of times a week. Hell, I used to put in some long hours, too, if you recall."

Chastised, Michael remembered numerous times when he'd wanted to talk to his father, and had to rely on his mother instead. She had never failed him. "You were always overloaded with cases."

Chuckling, Dan shifted in his seat. "Looks like you can stand some re-educating. 'Consciousness-raising,' your mother calls it. It's just a matter of changing how you look at something."

Michael gaped at his father. Consciousness-raising did not sound like Dan Jordan's cup of tea. Obviously he was dead serious. "What do you mean?"

"For your mother and me, our worst problems resulted from bad timing. She'd only had her accounting firm going six months when I retired from the Bureau. When it was essential for her to give most of her efforts to building a business, I had time on my hands, and not enough to fill it. You know I was grouchy and resentful, complaining to anyone who'd listen—mostly you. She had more pressing responsibilities than holding my hand. Instead of supporting her, I acted like a real bastard. I was used to her being available when I needed her, not the reverse." He pointed a finger at his son. "Sound familiar?"

Michael nodded, feeling the first stirrings of guilt, because he already knew the direction his father was headed in. If he hadn't been so self-absorbed, he'd have noticed the difference in his father before now. He did seem happier, more contented than he had since retiring.

"Finally, after months of tiptoeing around, trying to avoid my surliness, your mother got fed up and let me have it. It was one hell of a blowup, I'll tell you. Don't know where Bett picked up some of the colorful words she called me." His head moved from side to side at the memory.

"You two never argue, never fight."

Dan looked incredulous. "Son, all married couples fight. If they don't one of them is swallowing a load of anger. We just didn't do it in front of you kids."

"So you had a big row over her work, and your resentment of it?"

"Actually, it was more like Bett exploded and didn't give me a chance to do much but listen. Oh, I got to answer her questions—short answers, mostly."

"What did she ask?"

"Things like 'Dan, do you remember when Michael broke his arm? Or when Doug ran away? When Diana won her scholarship?'" Michael's father rubbed his chin. "You know, I had to think about every one of those events. And my recollections were hazy. I realized that I heard those facts over a long-distance phone line."

"What you did was important. Sometimes it meant life or death."

"That's the argument I offered. And guess what Bett said? She asked me if everyone else's lives were more important than those of my children. That brought me up short, son. Got me to thinking about all I missed. All the slack your mother took up without complaint. After I calmed down, I realized I owed her for over thirty years of handling all the crises by herself because my work was important."

"Now she's found something important to her and she wants you to return the favor," Michael said, remembering Ashley's words to that effect. Suddenly, the conclusion seemed so clear, so reasonable. Why hadn't he seen it before?

"It's only fair. For years, she was the constant in all our lives, and every one of us took advantage of it and took it for granted." Dan pawed through his tackle box and extracted an artificial lure before meeting his son's gaze straight on. "It's like this, Mike. A woman, even if she is a wife and mother, shouldn't have to do all the nurturing all the time. She ought to be able to have work that satisfies her, too. With a little help from her man, she can have that, along with marriage and children."

It's a myth that women can have it all. Ashley claimed to believe that. Michael couldn't accept it when doing so meant he would be deprived of everything he wanted. Love, marriage, a family—he needed them all, and only with Ashley.

Dan neatly tied on the red-and-white fly. "I didn't understand how much I depended on your mom until I was faced with the threat of losing her."

"Mom threatened to leave you?" Michael asked in a thick voice.

"She was at her wits' end. She was beginning to believe that was the one thing that would wake me up."

Michael remembered when his irritation with his mother had escalated into real anger. It had started when he first recognized that Ashley was different from the other women he'd known; that he wanted more from her. But she was an accountant, like his mother, and married to her job. Meaning she'd have neither the time nor the inclination to get involved with him. "I guess I thought that when I found the right woman, she'd be as ready and willing as I was."

Dan shrugged and made another cast. "Remember when you wanted that Eagle Scout badge? All the things you had to do to get it?"

He did, and he thought he understood the analogy his father was making. "Bottom line, Dad. I need advice."

"You love someone, that's all that counts. Everything else, you hang tough and work it out together. Don't ever lose sight of that."

Then Dan pinned his son with a piercing look. "Ever been in love before, Michael?"

"At thirty-four, I guess I've been in heat the normal amount of times in my life."

"Love?"

"Well, there have been a couple cases when I thought I might be."

"Love, son. Gut-wrenching, mind-twisting love?"

"Naw, there's never been anyone like Ashley. I don't think there ever will be."

"Ashley. I like it. Do I get to meet the young lady?"

"I think we'd better save that. I need time to get her used to the idea of having me around for the next fifty years or so. She's skittish, and even a simple introduction could send her into a panic. She'd probably read it—"

"As being looked over by a prospective father-in-law?"

"Exactly," Michael said, grinning as a wave of optimism flooded him. "Which, of course, it would be. She doesn't have to know that for a while longer."

"Your mother and I will be meeting her?"

"Count on it."

Dan looked all around him, a big smile crinkling his face. "Did I ever mention that I've always fancied the idea of teaching a few grandkids how to fish right here on this lake?"

Michael threw back his head and laughed, confident at last that he could trust his feelings and go after Ashley with no reservations. "I'll get to work on it right away, Dad."

9

ASHLEY PULLED INTO a visitor's parking spot in the lot adjoining Michael's condo. Was it a breach of company ethics to speak to Michael before she informed her superiors? They would have her hide if they ever found out. They might even fire her. Nonetheless, she was determined to go through with it, no matter what it cost her.

Ashley had worked alone all weekend, tracking down the details of the fraud that had taken place in the computer division last year. By telling Michael about what she'd uncovered, she was supplying him with what amounted to an advance warning.

She was doing the one thing she'd never imagined herself doing—risking her career for a man. Yet she would never be able to face her conscience if she didn't provide Michael with the opportunity to explain what had occurred under his supervision. She'd call company headquarters tomorrow. By then, she hoped, she wouldn't be regretting her departure from company policy.

Whatever happened next, Ashley knew she was at a crossroads. What she was about to do meant turning her back on the life she had so carefully made for herself—a life that had brought her satisfaction and security.

Turning off the engine, she retrieved her briefcase from the back seat and walked into the lobby of his condo. She got into the elevator and took it to the sixth floor. Her knock on his door was tentative. "Be right there," he called out. "Hang on."

She clutched the leather handles of her briefcase with both hands.

He opened the door, took in her rigid stance and pulled her inside. "Ashley. I'm glad you couldn't wait any longer, either. I was just getting ready to come after you."

He had on gray twill slacks, an unbuttoned gray-and-burgundy shirt, and was barefoot. Before she could be deflected by her feelings for him, she launched into a straightforward presentation of the facts.

"Michael, I think you ought to know the audit has revealed evidence of doctored invoices, purchase orders and delivery bills with regard to sales of hundred of personal computers stored in the Plymouth warehouse late last year."

He looked shocked, which was just as she'd expected. "This was a well-planned operation that allowed at least two people to divert hundreds of thousands of dollars into a dummy account."

"You're sure?"

"Positive. I've spent hours, days, on the paper trail."

His eyes narrowed. "Am I about to get a 'safe-guarding of assets' lecture?"

She didn't say a word.

"Is that why you're here, Ashley?" he pressed, his tone steely. "Do you want me to swear I had no part in the fraud?"

Hearing him speak those words filled her with relief. She hadn't come to accuse him. Nor did she need his guarantee that he had played no part in the scheme because she was certain he hadn't. She loved Michael, and the cornerstone of love was trust. Ashley believed in his bone-deep honesty and integrity. This man would never, ever, be guilty of anything illegal or unscrupulous.

"No," she said solemnly. "I didn't come for accusations or assurances."

Michael smiled a little at her admission, then barely touched the corner of her mouth with the tip of his index finger. His stern expression softened. "Why, then?"

The simplest reason for being here was professional concern for Michael, yet something even more basic than that had compelled her to come. She'd missed him dreadfully. Each day, the need to be with him had grown stronger, making it impossible to stay away. Since that only complicated matters, she hedged. "I don't know why I'm here."

"I think you do. You just don't want to tell me." His hands reached around her to the small of her back, and pulled.

"Michael, stop!" A second tug brought her close enough to feel his heat. "This is serious."

"At least we agree on that much." He pulled again, fusing them together.

"What are you doing?" she wailed. He was strong and determined.

"In accountant's terms, so you'll understand it, I'm making a consolidated statement." One arm holding her captive, he plucked an anchoring pin from the twist on the back of her head. Dropping it to the floor he then systematically removed every pin until her hair spilled over his fingers.

"You have to listen to me."

"Oh, I will, honey. I will. I love hearing those soft, sweet sounds you make when you take me inside." Beneath the jacket of her beige linen suit, his palms curved over her shoulders, lifted, and efficiently stripped it down her arms. It landed in a crumpled heap on the floor beside them.

He peeled his shirt off and flung it atop her jacket. "I'm one up on you already," he said hoarsely, bringing her hand to his bare torso while he traced the embossed flowers on her peach satin camisole.

Ashley's fingers tracked the muscular ridges of his rib cage before she yanked them back and clasped her hands tightly together. He was so taut, such a delicious contrast to her that she yearned to explore their differences again, but didn't dare. "You can't do this," she protested, as the button on her skirt gave way and she felt the fabric slide down over her slip into a ring at her feet. Just as quickly, his slacks followed the same path.

What she meant was that she shouldn't allow him to do this.

She'd come to terms with the idea that what she and Michael had shared should end. This was her last chance to store up memories, so she was going to seize it without guilt or remorse. When Michael grasped the hem of her camisole, she reveled in the feel of his hands skimming the silk over her head.

He reached behind her and switched off the bright overhead light, turning the atmosphere shadowy and intimate. Michael was normally talkative when they made love; tonight she found his silent stripping of her exquisitely provocative. It clearly had the same effect on him. Ashley regarded his powerful arousal when he stepped out of his dark briefs.

Standing naked before him, bathed in the glow of distant city lights, she felt transformed. Surely the woman in the mirror opposite them couldn't be her. He had hardly touched her, hadn't kissed her, yet her body was attuned to his, warm and yielding, ready to accept him.

At first she'd condemned him for being a jock, disparaging all his physical activities on principle. Now she blessed every exercise he had ever done to make him into the sleek, tensile male animal that stood before her. She searched for an adequate word to describe him, settling on *magnificent*. "You are magnificent," she murmured.

He guided her fingers along the hard length of his erection. "What I am is obvious."

"I may not be as obvious, but I need you just as much."

"You want me to carry you up the stairs?"

"I don't think I can wait that long."

"The couch?"

"No." In perfect silent communication, they sank to the rug, and after that, the only sound was the blending of their raw, incoherent cries of passion.

ASHLEY WASN'T SURE how much time had passed since their mating downstairs. She didn't even know how they'd gotten up the steps and onto the four-poster, or where her clothes were. She now wore his shirt and he had pulled on a pair of gym shorts. She had no memory beyond her reckless quest for oblivion and Michael's feverish race to find it with her. On the floor, no less.

They'd both been wild, demanding, driven to the edge of consciousness. Possessed.

"I used to joke about not letting my pleasures kill me," Ashley murmured against his damp chest. "I didn't really think it was possible . . . until you."

He said nothing, but his arms bound her to him so tightly that she allowed herself the brief fantasy of having their strong, loving support permanently.

"To think I lived twenty-eight years and never knew how elemental, how consuming, sex is."

"Sex isn't."

She went numb, aware on some instinctual level that they were approaching a turning point. "I'm not sure what you mean."

"My time is running out, and now you've come up with this other indictment against me. I have to make my move." He turned her to face him, framing her chin in the brace of his thumb and forefinger. "Ashley, I love you."

"No, don't say that! You can't!" she sobbed.

"Can't say it?"

She got out of bed and stumbled over to the dresser, keeping her back to him. "No, can't do it. Don't love me."

"Why?"

"You haven't known me long enough."

He realized she was skirting the real issue. "Not long by the calendar, maybe, but I've discovered that love doesn't come to you in small increments, like when you're accumulating a stock portfolio. It might strike unexpectedly, but trust me, when it does, you know."

And she did. Loving Michael had complicated her life, compromised her professionally and made her dread a future without him. Ashley believed him. She also believed he loved her—now—because he didn't truly know her or anything about her background. Over time, he'd discover how unsuited she was for his version of "happily ever after." She knew she couldn't bear his disappointment and rejection when that time came. Better for both of them that she rebuff him now.

"You said it yourself: I'm a big girl. I made a choice. Don't feel you have to promise undying love because we slept together a few times. You're in the grip of lust. Don't mistake that for something stronger. You can't really love me."

"Well, sweetheart, that's where you're wrong. I do love you. And what's more, I want us to get married. As soon as we can."

Ashley turned to face him. He wasn't going to let her escape without her baring her soul. "Michael, you have to understand. I've tried to tell you all along that whatever we have together can only last a matter of weeks."

"Why?"

"I'm not expected to marry."

"'Not expected to'—what the hell does that mean?"

She had known from the beginning that he was different, that in some way, she would come to grief because of him. Talk about time running out. Ashley mouthed a silent plea that she'd be able to say her piece objectively, and that Michael would finally accept it. "For two centuries—probably longer—every generation of Atwoods has had at least one maiden aunt. In mine, it's me."

Michael looked appalled, as if she'd just confessed to a particularly grisly crime. She hurried on, anxious to get through the tale. "I may not have what it takes to catch a husband, but there's a certain satisfaction in knowing my aunts are successful in their chosen careers. I'm sure I'll manage quite well, too."

He got out of bed and snagged Ashley's wrist. With her in tow, he stalked down the hall to the other room. Taking possession of the rowing machine, he began pumping away. Each stroke sent ripples across his back, shoulders, chest and arms. She stared at the overt display of sinewy strength until she realized he was watching her.

"Want to give it a try?" he asked with a hint of challenge.

It appeared she was going to be spared any further grilling. "Uh, no thanks. I'll pass. But you make it look easy."

"Lots of practice. I got interested in rowing as a team sport when we moved here, and made varsity crew in college." He did another series of strokes, inhaling and exhaling in time. "I still belong to a rowing club, and since we compete in several regattas every year, I try to keep in shape."

She'd have been content to watch his smooth, synchronized movements forever.

"How is this aunt selected, Ashley? I mean, why are you the one?"

"Genetic predetermination. What else?" Ashley had come to terms with her fate. "I can't explain it, but I've always known I'm like Aunt Kitty, who was like Great-Aunt Fan, and before her, Eula."

"You say you're like them. In what way?"

She shrugged, skipping her fingers along his eclectic album collection. "In the early sixties, Kitty fled Charleston and moved to New York. She started her own advertising agency, and if that wasn't crass enough, she succeeded. In a big way. The family puts her in the same category as those rabid used-car salesmen in television commercials."

She wouldn't have become enmeshed in this emotional tangle if she'd been able to reach Kitty but it was too late to lament her aunt's mysterious disappearance. "Atwood women are supposed to be charming and refined, skilled at tea pouring and do-gooding. Above all, they don't clutter up their heads with business matters or, the ultimate heresy, try to support themselves. That's men's work."

Ashley crossed her arms, though it wasn't easy to sound accountant-like while wearing only an oversize shirt. "Kitty never married or got seriously involved with a man. Yet she has a full, exciting life by herself, for herself."

Michael made a mocking sound. Undaunted, Ashley continued, "A generation earlier, Great-Aunt Fan, against legions of male advice, took charge of her inheritance and astounded everyone by quadrupling it on the stock market. Eula ran off to the Continent, where she organized and conducted a chamber orchestra."

Michael continued to row, his glistening, nearly nude body mesmerizing Ashley. "How many more ancestresses would you like to hear about?"

He halted his rowing and grabbed a towel. "Well, Ash, that's a real entertaining story. Eula, Fan, Kitty—

fascinating ladies, I'm sure. But, last names aside, I don't see that they have a damn thing to do with you."

DURING THE REMAINDER of that manic week and through the next, Ashley thought about Michael's pronouncement in her free moments—not that she had many of those. Monday evening, after repeatedly trying to make him see the logic of her maiden-aunt theory, she'd left in frustration. Nothing she said would convince him.

In the final analysis it didn't matter if he bought the "myth" as he called it, or not. She had bigger obstacles facing her than one man's stubbornness. Ashley had sat up until the wee hours of Tuesday morning outlining her work plan.

It was irregular and would probably require the examination of someone higher up the corporate ladder than the person she usually reported to. No audit she'd ever done had turned up a large-scale fraud. Ashley intended to capitalize on her killer-mole reputation to ensure that she got the assignment, along with carte blanche to handle it as she saw fit.

Knowing what she had to do, she packed her small bag, left a message with the hotel desk for Jack and Mark, swung by the office to drop off a letter she'd written to Michael, then caught a red-eye to Atlanta. Her co-workers were instructed to wind up the audit by on-site examination of the Plymouth warehouse and a stock count. She hoped the few hints in her note to Michael would be sufficient to pacify him until she could complete her investigation.

By late morning of her first day back at the head office Ashley had repeated her story three times—to the director of operations, executive vice president and the CEO. Before she dragged herself home that night, her strategy for finding the guilty parties had not only been authorized, it had been given the seal of approval by none other than Glenn Cousins, the CEO himself.

By then she was so exhausted, she was operating on autopilot. Skipping dinner, she went to bed at eight. Sleep was more crucial than food. She had to wake energized and prepared to face the rigors awaiting her. She was fighting for the man she loved, and nothing but her best would do.

She couldn't agree to the marriage Michael claimed to want—not with the certainty that he'd soon change his mind about her. But she could leave him with something valuable: she could run the real culprits in his business to the ground and save his reputation.

Ashley felt more like a detective than an auditor. She liked the feeling. While her accountant's orderly thought processes came in handy, this task was a lot more interesting than juggling numbers day after day.

She'd been too inflexible, too bent on subduing her freethinking self in order to defy her family. After all these years she'd proved everything—to them and to herself. What would it matter if she took off in a new direction? There was nothing to prevent her from branching out. People changed career directions every day, and so could she. But not yet. . . .

By MIDAFTERNOON of the second Friday, Michael found himself glancing at his open door every few minutes. He'd been expecting Ashley all day and the waiting was beginning to eat at him. It had taken only a few weeks for him to get used to having her close every day.

Not that he hadn't known where she was, what she was up to, almost every hour since her abrupt departure. In twelve years with the company, he'd built up an extensive internal network. A few phone calls and he could find out almost anything he wanted to know.

From the moment she'd started her whirlwind siege of the Atlanta headquarters, Michael had her figured out. He'd even done some sleuthing himself at the local end, and had wound up on the same trail as Ashley.

He was encouraged and moved by the notion of Ashley's championing of his cause.

Despite the seriousness of the fraud, Michael hadn't reacted as precipitately as she had. There was no way he personally could be found culpable.

"Excuse me, Mr. Jordan," his secretary said, "Ms. Atwood is here to see you."

Michael got up, annoyed that after watching for her all day, she'd sneaked in while he was lost in thought. "Thanks, Carol. I've been expecting her. Send her in and—"

"I know. Hold your calls." Carol motioned Ashley inside, then discreetly closed the door behind her.

He gestured toward a chair, waiting until she sat down before claiming his own. "So, Ms. Atwood, I hear you've been busy the past two weeks. You had quite a few people at headquarters jumping through hoops."

When Ashley realized he'd known not only her whereabouts, but actions, too, she pursed her lips in prissy indignation.

Now, that was what a maiden aunt should look like, Michael reflected. The Ashley he knew couldn't quite pull it off.

"So much for secrecy," she said, clearly irritated. "And so much for trying to do you a favor," she added under her breath.

"I told you once, I have pipelines to the right people." It was so good to have her back that Michael couldn't resist some mild teasing. He liked Ashley's spirit and enjoyed coaxing her into revealing it. He saw that he had to go easy on her today. She looked beat. She'd pushed herself past exhaustion yet he was exhilarated because she had. It had to mean she loved him—he hoped.

She gripped the arms of her chair, as if she needed their help to stand. "I guess you already know everything I came to tell you. I've wasted a trip."

"Take it easy," he said. "I only know the basic approach you took, not your conclusions." That wasn't one-hundred-percent true, but close enough. He did want to hear it all from her. "Give me the whole story."

Ashley sighed. Sitting seemed to have deflated her. "I'll just give you a quick rundown. You can read all the details when I've finished my report."

"Fair enough," he agreed, wanting to get out of there as quickly as possible so he could take care of her. She looked as if she needed pampering, and he needed to do it.

"I examined your personnel, to see who was in a position to actually plan and carry out the operation. It had to be a joint effort, and the most likely places to check were order entry, shipping and receiving."

Listening to her, Michael's morale soared. She'd gone to extraordinary lengths for him.

"Then I cross-checked a computer profile of workers in both those departments for a year prior to and following the disappearance, with an eye out for new employees and terminations. It was amazing how two characters practically leaped off the pages, shouting 'It was me!' After that, it was just a matter of pulling their individual files and running a follow-up."

"So you're sure who it was?"

"Yes. You have to hand it to these guys—they're clever. Before coming to work for us, they ripped off a competitor, then applied for jobs with us, complete with recommendations."

"Clever," Michael conceded. "But con men all the same."

"Indeed. In both instances they must have known the schedules for inventory as well as internal audits."

Michael transferred the papers from his desk into a drawer and locked it. "What's next?"

Ashley assumed he was referring to the culprits and not their personal situation. "We bring in the fraud division."

"How did you like detective work, Ash? A little more challenging than auditing, maybe?"

He'd meant it as a jest, but she squirmed in her seat.

"I don't plan to switch occupations anytime soon," she said stiffly. "I have almost a whole year remaining on my contract."

"Still, it's something to think about, isn't it? Most auditors would have written up a report and dumped it in someone else's lap." He picked up a gold fountain pen, examined it carefully, then pointed it at her. "You, however, rush off to play Nancy Drew. Why?"

Ashley turned to the side in her chair, as if she didn't care to face him head-on. "It was clear to me that what I found was significant enough to warrant quick action."

He gave her his warmest, most reassuring smile. "What was the real reason, Ashley?"

He was pushing, and she knew for what. That was the one thing she couldn't handle in her present state. "My reasons are my own—not up for discussion.

You'll get a copy of the final report. As you once said, there's nothing to hang you with there. Everything will go back to the way it was before the audit."

"Nothing will be the same, and you know it."

Ashley felt trapped, and knew she must be telegraphing her distress.

"What are you planning to do now?"

"Pack my bags and catch the last flight out to Charleston for Kitty's birthday party tomorrow night." She rose, reeling from fatigue. "If I survive that, I'm going to rush back to my apartment in Atlanta, unplug the phone, hang a Do Not Disturb sign on my door and sleep for a month."

"What about me?"

"I guess you can sleep for a month, too, if you like."

"Don't you dare use that flippant debutante routine on me, Ashley." Uncoiling from his chair, with the swiftness of a serpent, he grasped her shoulders and gave her a slight shake. "Do you think I can be dismissed as easily as a servant?"

Ashley paled. "I didn't mean that."

His grip eased, his voice softened. "I didn't either, sweetheart. I'm sorry. You're dead on your feet, and all because of me. I shouldn't be hassling you." He turned her toward the door, slipping his arm around her waist. "Look, don't decide anything, don't do anything until you've rested. Let me drive you to the hotel. Get a few hours sleep and we'll talk later. Okay?"

"There's really only one thing left to say, Michael, and I need to do it here, right now."

His arm tensed, and she heard him swallow.

"What's that?"

"Goodbye."

10

I HAVE TO GET OUT OF HERE!

Ashley had been repeating that silent litany ever since escaping Michael's office. He hadn't come after her, but that didn't mean she could breathe easy. She didn't think he was the type to let her walk away with only a single word of farewell. Michael would figure—rightly so—that he deserved more. She didn't have the stamina to face him at the moment. Maybe in a few weeks, when she got her life back under control, she'd call and have a long talk with him.

She dashed back and forth between the armoire and two open suitcases on her bed, tossing in suits, blouses and lingerie without regard for the fine fabrics. Dimly aware that everything wasn't going to fit in if she didn't do a neater job, Ashley continued her haphazard attempt at packing. Nothing mattered except getting away.

"Running out on me, Ash?"

She started at the sound of Michael's voice behind her, and a handful of shoes went flying in all directions. "How did you get in here?" she demanded, eyeing the key in his hand. "Who gave you that?"

"It was in the door. In your haste I guess you forgot and left it there. Careless of you, convenient for me." Shaking his head, he extricated a balled silk blouse crammed into one corner of her suitcase. "In case you're wondering, though, I'd have kicked in the door if necessary."

Ashley leaned against the wall. "Why can't you just let it go, Michael? We knew this day would come."

"That's your line, and I'm not buying it. Nor did I come to hear any more of your twisted rationalizations about maiden aunts and marriage. We have more urgent issues to be dealt with."

"Such as?"

"Such as that night you showed up at my condo."

She blushed at the memory of what had taken place in the entry hall. The interlude might have been a dream except that she'd carried the marks of their mutual passion for several days afterward.

"I was coming to see you, but hadn't finished dressing. You caught me . . . unprepared." He ran his palm from her throat to her waist, then lower. "I might have made you pregnant, Ashley."

She jerked aside, stricken, one hand going automatically to her stomach. "No! That's impossible!"

"Is it?"

Of course it wasn't. The first time they'd been together, she'd relied on him to take care of birth control. The occasion he was talking about had been spontaneous. Uncontrollable. It represented an obligation she would never force on Michael. In a shaky voice, she said, "If I'm pregnant, I accept full responsibility. I'll handle it myself." But—oh, God—how?

"No, Ashley. You will not handle it by yourself."

She didn't have the strength to resist when he steered her toward the bed, disposed of the luggage and flung back the covers. "From now on, everything you do concerns me. For however long it takes to get that through your head, I'm prepared to keep hammering away. But not now. Until you've had some rest, you are not going anywhere or making any decisions."

He tenderly undressed her, worked a nightshirt over her head and stretched her out on the cool sheets. "Sleep, Ashley," he said softly. "I'll be here when you wake up."

Exhausted, she drifted off, with his last words, "I'll be here," inside her head.

When she woke, Ashley blearily focused on the bedside clock. It was after eleven—she'd missed her plane. She could hear Eleanor Atwood now, scolding her because she'd failed to show up at the arranged time. How could she have let go like that and allowed Michael to take over? She tried to feel angry and resentful, but to be honest, she'd been a barely mobile zombie before stealing a few hours sleep. Now that she was capable of coherent thought, she could come up with a more civilized parting speech, providing he was still there. Otherwise, she'd sneak off as originally planned.

She groped her way to the bathroom, feeling revitalized after brushing her teeth and splashing cool water on her face. When she turned off the tap, she heard him moving around in the front part of the suite. Still there, as promised. Tired, and famished because she'd eaten nothing since early morning, Ashley steeled herself to do battle with Michael for what she hoped would be the last time. Neither of them stood to gain by endlessly rehashing the same overworked arguments and rebuttals.

She found him in the tiny pullman kitchen, whistling. "What's this?"

"I guessed you'd be hungry, so while you slept I went out and picked up a few things. Sit."

She ambled over to the small round table in the corner, watching him microwave a bowl of broccoli cheese soup, which he paired with a smoked turkey and sprout sandwich. He set the plate and a glass of milk in front of her, then went back to the refrigerator. "Eat every bite," he instructed, "and you get a treat."

Ashley drooled. He was tempting her with French silk pie from Baker's Square, another guilty pleasure she'd become addicted to in Minneapolis. The man didn't fight fair. He even stood guard over the pie, not letting her sneak a bite until she'd polished off the nourishing food.

It was then that she saw his garment bag spread out on the couch. "Going somewhere?" she inquired, fearing his answer.

"We have a flight tomorrow, to Charleston through Charlotte."

He made the "we" sound like a dare. Ashley jumped up, the tasty food she'd devoured a brick in her stomach. "I'd think about that if I were you. Take it from me, if Kitty's birthday party wasn't a tradition, I'd stay as far away from that place as possible."

"Are they really such monsters?"

She gave a short, hollow laugh. "If you were introduced to them, I'm sure they'd all greet you with excruciating politeness. You might even find them gracious. Underlying the surface charm, there would be a smidgen of condescension because they don't know your people. My mother and sister do great condescension. They're so good at it, most of their victims don't realize they've been patronized."

"You're one of the family. Surely they don't treat you that way."

"No, worse. I receive scorn because I'm supposed to know how to act." Ashley drifted to the window and pushed the drape aside to stare out at the atrium. Without thinking, she recited the familiar speech, unconsciously adopting Eleanor's accent, which had a far more pronounced drawl that her own. "Breeding and a sense of what is correct and proper will never be out of fashion. Until you learn that, Ashley, you will not be accepted in the most desirable circles. You're doomed to be alone and unloved, as surely as Kitty is."

She turned back to Michael, forcing a smile. "Do you know, that's probably my first memory." She crossed her arms, drawing them close to her midsection. "I'd defied Mother over something silly like dancing shoes or piano lessons. Later I overheard her tell my father, 'Ah declare, Charles, there's no hope for Ashley. She's just like Kitty. We'll never be able to make a decent match for her.' She'd already written me off and I must have been all of five or six. In case I didn't get the message then, she repeated it so often that even a slow learner would have grasped it."

Before she could go on, Michael moved across the room and had his arms clamped around her, pressing her head to his shoulder, smoothing her tangled hair. Here it was, at last; the real reason Ashley was so certain she'd never get married. Her mother had drilled it into her that she was unlovable, undesirable, that no man would ever *want* to marry her. Out of self-preservation, Ashley had talked herself into believing she neither needed nor wanted a husband. The maiden-aunt nonsense was just a cover-up, a face-saving justification. She'd endured years of confidence-destroying verbal attacks because she refused to be molded into an Eleanor Atwood clone. It made Michael fighting mad.

"Ashley, sweetheart, your mother doesn't know her ass from a hole in the ground."

She laughed, genuinely this time. "I'm sure she'd be delighted to hear that. It would almost be worth taking you along if you'd promise to deliver your opinion in those precise words."

"You think I won't?"

His ferocity seemed to jolt her. "I was only joking. I wouldn't really expect you to lock horns with Eleanor Boone Atwood."

"Don't you understand that I'd take on Lucifer himself in defense of you? Because I know the real you, and nobody could be more lovable, more desirable. I'm the expert on this, so you have to trust what I'm saying. You had me down for the count the minute I found you in that flooded parking lot. I've been falling a little bit more in love every day since then."

Tears sprang to her eyes. She blinked them back. "I told you, I'm not looking for love."

She expected anger. What she got was tenderness. Gentle caresses, soft words, softer kisses. "Yes, you are. You want it and need it but your heart's tied up. You're afraid to feel because of what somebody has convinced you will never happen. It's a crock."

"Do you ever give up?"

"Why should I when I have too much to lose? I love you, Ashley. I'll do whatever it takes to prove how much. Forget 'correct and proper' and all the people who think that has anything to do with being acceptable. It's your mother who needs to be sent a message. I'm going to Charleston with you to see that she gets it. That's the final word on the subject."

And Ashley believed him.

They slept together all night, as close as any two people could be. Michael was content to hold her. Though Ashley would have welcomed his lovemaking, she was on too shaky ground emotionally to initiate it.

She went to sleep and woke with the same resolution. She'd tried every other avenue, and they had all failed. Might as well let him go to Charleston and see firsthand what a misfit she was.

That would demolish his illusions more effectively than anything she could say.

ASHLEY GREW STEADILY quieter as their rental car neared the waterfront. Her only words were clipped directions to the East Battery. From every window of the splendid old house, a warm, golden glow greeted them. Michael could tell by the tension in Ashley's voice and posture that she didn't feel welcome. Her hand shook as she reached for the bell.

The door swung open at once, as if the tiny old woman had been waiting for them. "My baby," she exclaimed, throwing her arms around Ashley in an exuberant hug. "Let me look at you." She backed away and studied her critically. "Too skinny, as usual. You need to come home and let me fatten you up some. Bet you ain' had biscuits and grits in months."

Her curious eyes, sharp beacons shining out of a dark face, settled on Michael. Without shifting her gaze, she asked Ashley, "Who might this gentleman be?"

"Bessie, this is Michael Jordan. He's from Minnesota and works for the same company as I do. Michael, Bessie Davis, my friend for as long as I can remember."

"Mr. Jordan, welcome to Charleston," Bessie said formally.

"Michael, please. Maybe you'll share some of your recipes. I've been trying to fatten her up, as you put it, for over a month."

Dark eyes studied him skeptically. "You cook?" The idea of a man cooking for a woman was clearly beyond her.

"He's a wonderful cook, Bessie," Ashley put in. "Almost as good as you."

"Humph," Bessie replied, shaking her head. Then she inclined it toward a closed door and frowned. "They all in there. Might as well go on in, I reckon."

Michael watched Ashley draw in a single deep breath and straighten her back. He couldn't imagine having to fortify himself to see his family. Her dread was obvious. He touched her shoulder lightly in support and she patted his hand before walking to the door.

The instant she grasped the polished brass lever, a mellow male voice commanded, "Come in, Ashley. We've been waiting for you."

It was like a tribal council. Surrounded by a century and a half of polished elegance, the five subjects, already dressed for the party, trained their collective gazes on the new arrivals. The man and woman seated in brocade wing chairs would be Ashley's parents, the younger couple, her sister and brother-in-law. A third woman stood behind one of the wing chairs. Decked out in a flamboyant red beaded jumpsuit, this had to be the notorious Aunt Kitty. Chin propped on one hand, a faint smile playing around her mouth, she evaluated him.

Her amusement grew when she told her niece, "Ashley, you look like you're poised on the edge of a snake pit. Why not plunge right in and let the vipers have at you?"

"Why not?" Ashley agreed, reaching for Michael's hand before advancing into the room. With perfect manners, she introduced each in turn.

Ashley's mother remained seated. Regal as a queen, she smiled and dipped her head in acknowledgment, as if he were a loyal subject. Eleanor looked as delicate as an orchid. Michael sensed her gentility was a deceptive facade. Though she would never be so gauche as to say so, he could see her marveling at his nerve in showing up there without an engraved invitation.

Tall, dignified and silver-haired, Charles Atwood offered a firm handshake, seeming perplexed by Michael's presence. He looked back and forth between Michael and Ashley several times, then kissed her on the cheek.

Cooper and her husband, Reynolds Lee, transmitted their dismissal of him as someone of no consequence. He could hardly keep from laughing aloud. The one thing guaranteed to elevate Michael in Ashley's eyes would be her family's rejection of him.

Impatient with the proceedings, Kitty moved to speed things along. "Katherine Atwood, Michael. How brave of you to join us." Her grip was strong, businesslike; her eyes, mischievous. She obviously enjoyed taking pot shots at her relatives' pomposity. "Call me Kitty, don't ask my age and we'll get on splendidly."

He guessed she had sized him up and decided his intentions were honorable. Michael made snap decisions about people in the same way, and he had quickly pegged Kitty as an ally whose help he might need before the night was over. While Ashley slept during the long plane ride, he'd mulled over his options. There was only one that appealed to Michael's preference for action. Chancy as it was, he had to force her into making a choice, and hope it turned out in his favor.

With the formalities completed, Ashley hustled him out of the parlor. The party was scheduled to begin in less than an hour and they were both wearing jeans—a fact that had not escaped anyone's attention.

"I hope that wasn't too horrible for you," she fretted as they climbed the stairs and she showed him into a guest room. "They can be so rigid at times."

"Don't worry about me, Ash. As you're always telling me, I can take care of myself." The Atwoods didn't intimidate him at all. He found Ashley's solicitude telling. On the plane he'd figured out the cause of her willingness to let him come here with her. Now that she understood her hang-up, it wasn't difficult to follow her pattern of behavior. She thought that if he saw her with her family, saw how she didn't fit in, he'd reach the same conclusion her mother had: that she was unsuitable for marriage.

Instead he'd had the opposite reaction. He admired and loved her more for her vitality and resilience. Michael had grown up in the security of a loving, accepting family. He could only imagine the kind of inner strength Ashley must have to emerge from her upbringing with any self-confidence at all. She had, and despite all their differences, he wanted to spend the rest of his life showing her how well matched the two of them were.

If love counted for anything, he could do it.

FOR THE FIRST PART of the evening Ashley stayed within arm's length of Michael. There were over a hundred people here. There was no way she was going to leave him at the mercy of so many strangers. She had to admit he was handling Charleston's best quite well. Because he didn't have a need to impress anybody, he impressed everybody. The men seemed interested in what he had to say, and the women were just . . . interested. They were probably all wondering how Ashley had captured the attention of such a delectable, eligible male. How many times had she wondered the same thing?

Several hours into the festivities, Ashley caught Michael staring at her.

"What are you doing?" she whispered, putting herself between him and the crowd.

"Thinking about throwing you over my shoulder and charging up that free-flying staircase to the nearest bedroom." His smile was so lascivious, she felt a familiar moistness. "Give 'em something to talk about over their morning coffee."

"You wouldn't dare!"

His smile promised he *would* dare that, and a great deal more. Ashley went hot. She wished she had borrowed her Great-Aunt Julia's trademark ivory-and-peacock feather fan. "You really should try to spend a little time with Kitty if you can. I think you'd find talking with her, uh, informative."

"If you're trying to get rid of me, say no more. I've been thinking along those same lines, myself. I'm sure I'll learn a lot."

That was why she'd made the suggestion in the first place. She watched him weave his way through the crowd to Kitty's side. The two of them disappeared into the library, shutting the door behind them. If Michael heard the truth from a third party, he would give it more credence and finally accept what she'd told him so many times.

As the night wore on, Ashley grew anxious. Simply being here in this house, among these people, invoked painful memories. Normally, Kitty was her anchor at affairs like this. Now even her aunt was inaccessible. Most disturbing was the situation with Michael, building toward its irrevocable climax. She felt like a heroine in a Greek tragedy, unable to alter what fate had decreed.

Great glory! Now she was turning melodramatic—a sure sign the whole scene was getting to her. Ashley headed for the lavish buffet in the dining room. If she stuffed her face, she could get by with a minimum of the inane small talk that varied little from year to year. What this group needed was an injection of fresh blood. Somebody to shake them up a bit. Someone like Michael. She swallowed three crab puffs in quick succession, then checked again to see if the library door remained closed. What on earth could her aunt and Michael have to say that would take forty-five minutes?

Whatever it was, made him look grim and resolved. On the other hand, Kitty looked smug and pleased with herself. Ashley was plain puzzled when Michael came straight to her, taking her arm firmly as he propelled her out the French doors onto the piazza. "I need to talk to you. It won't take long."

Ashley felt the strength of his implacable will, and a chill slithered along her spine. Her evening sandals clicked against the patterned brick of the terrace, the rapid beat increasing in time with her heart's. Something momentous was about to occur and all she could do was follow Michael into the garden, waiting for him to deal the final blow. She told herself she'd expected it, that it was for the best. It ought not to hurt this much.

From inside torchères, candlelight flickered over the harsh set of his features, revealing the determination there. He didn't speak until she sat on a wrought-iron bench. In contrast to the warm, heavy air, the metal felt cool through her dress and against her bare back. Michael stood, hands clasped behind him, staring at the astrolabe in the center of the garden.

"Ashley, I brought you out here to tell you I'm leaving. Now. I guess I shouldn't have come at all."

She'd had weeks to prepare herself. She wasn't ready. Pride dictated that she accept this without blubbering like a baby, which was what she really felt like doing. "I did try telling you not to come, but you wouldn't listen. I warned you about these folks."

"My going has nothing to do with anyone else. This is between you and me, where it's been all along."

"I see," she said. "I knew Kitty would be able to get through to you. She's very good at selling concepts as well as products."

"Your aunt told me a great many things. Most of it would surprise you, but none of it changed my mind about anything except leaving right away."

Baffled, Ashley stared at him.

He moved closer, going down on one knee in front of her. "Here it is, Ash: my final statement. I can smother you with love. I want to. First you have to come to terms with what *you* need and want. Until you take a good look at that, there's not much I can do. So I'm going to leave you alone and let you make up your mind without pressure from me." He squeezed her clenched hands once. "Truth is, I'm tired of butting up against the same impenetrable wall."

Ashley bowed her head, wishing she could deny blame for Michael's pain and disillusionment. He didn't deserve to be hurt by anyone, least of all her. Not when he'd given her so much.

"Please st—" slipped out before she checked the plea. No, she couldn't beg him to stay.

Using only the tip of his index finger, he lifted her face to catch the moon's soft brilliance. Then he broke a gardenia blossom off the bush next to the bench. Without touching her, he dropped the flower into the cleavage of her strapless dress.

"Think about what we can have together." He lowered his lips to touch the gardenia. "Think about *me*, Ashley Atwood, in the dead of night when there's no one else who knows what you need." His mouth brushed the upper curve of her breasts. "And think about how lonely your life's going to be if I'm not in it."

11

ASHLEY SLUMPED against the bench, battling an awesome sense of abandonment. The gardenia's cloying scent sickened her and she hurled the blossom away. From now on, she'd associate the smell of gardenias with the loss of Michael. Fighting the urge to cry, she walked briskly to the gazebo by the back wall. She sank onto a seat and rested her forehead on the surrounding rail. "You asked for this," she admonished herself bitterly. "You knew what would happen, and you didn't stop." Now she was faced with the agony of separation.

Ashley gave up and let the first tears trickle down her cheeks. She sat motionless until the bells at St. Michael's chimed midnight, then she cried harder. Strange that she noticed them now—those bells that had measured a good portion of her life. Generations of Atwoods had been christened, married and eulogized in St. Michael's. It was as much a part of their heritage as the house on East Battery. She had never felt more an outsider than she did at that moment.

Sounds of celebration, applause and cheers, intruded on her reflections. That would be the traditional toast to Kitty's birthday, proposed by Ashley's father, continued by friends and finally, a last toast by Kitty herself which brought the fete to a close.

Avoiding everyone, she crept into the kitchen, liberated a bottle of chilled champagne and escaped up the rear stairs to her bedroom. She'd missed toasting her aunt's birthday. She wasn't feeling very contrite. Had Kitty been where she was supposed to be, she might have spared Ashley this anguish.

Several glassfuls later, an aggressive knock shook her door. "I'm asleep," Ashley mumbled from a comfortable sprawl on her bed. She hadn't bothered to take off the dress, since she planned never to wear it again.

"Asleep, huh?" Kitty commented from the open doorway.

"Thought I'd locked that." Ashley blinked against an exhaustion- and champagne-induced haze.

"Obviously not." Her aunt swept into the room, pushed the door shut and turned the key. "Must have been one terrible day," she said, eyeing the champagne level in the bottle.

"The absolute worst day of my life." Ashley refilled her glass with unsteady hands and clunked the bottle onto her nightstand, heedless of the interlocking rings of moisture it left on the surface.

"Think all that champagne will help?"

"Till tomorrow."

Kitty whisked away the bottle and headed for the bathroom. Ashley heard the bubbly fizzing and glugging as it was poured down the drain. "I realize we've been out of touch for a while. In the meantime, I didn't expect you to turn into a self-pitying whiner."

"You're supposed to sympathize with my misery," Ashley complained, not really expecting that tender emotion from her pragmatic relative.

"Okay, spill it. Don't waste my time with protests."

Ashley thought she'd cried her limit out in the garden, but her eyes began to smart again. "I should have known it was too good to be true. I did know."

Kitty sat on the edge of the bed and asked, "Know what?"

"That no man, especially one as outstanding as Michael, could find anything about me to love."

Kitty lay her hand on Ashley's shoulder. "Darling, the funny thing about love is that it doesn't always have a rational explanation. That's why you should accept it as a marvelous gift—not necessarily because you earned it, but because you're lucky enough to find it. Take it from one who knows."

Ashley glanced up from the tissue she had twisted into a rope. She'd never seen her aunt smile with such radiance. All the strange vibes she'd been feeling about Kitty for weeks returned with a surge. "What's going on?"

"If you hadn't sneaked away to mope, you'd know."

"Well, I did, and I don't. So are you going to tell me?"

Kitty smiled with doting indulgence. "Of course, I am. You see, not only did you miss toasting my birthday, you also missed toasting my marriage."

Ashley's ears rang. Her body went numb. She watched the glass slide from her fingers. Champagne soaked her black taffeta dress. "Married! I don't believe it. That's impossible."

"On the contrary." As proof, Kitty flashed a filegreed band, an exquisite pairing of emeralds and diamonds.

"You eloped!" Ashley gasped, absorbing the reason Kitty had been unavailable to answer her desperation calls. "Who? When? Why?"

"Why should be obvious. The wedding was May first, then we stole away for a long honeymoon before telling anyone. And his name is Richard Hathaway."

"But I thought . . . everyone assumed . . . you always seemed . . . Oh, dear. I'm making a mess of this. I'm supposed to say 'Congratulations.' No, no. That's for the groom. Help!"

Kitty laughed at Ashley's confusion. "Can you imagine the uproar when I announced this instead of my toast? There was a pause, absolute silence, then the place erupted. Bet you've never seen your mother struck dumb. I'll cherish the memory for years."

"This is too much to comprehend." Ashley righted her glass and put it on the nightstand. "Why isn't he here?"

"Richard's with the U.N., and he had a trip to Europe that couldn't be rescheduled, so he left early this morning. I miss him awfully." She took the crumpled tissue from Ashley's hand. "Know the feeling?"

"Unfortunately, yes." She reached for another tissue. "At least yours is temporary. Michael's gone for good."

"Says who? Did he say goodbye? Tell you he never wanted to see you again? Don't bother answering, because I already know he didn't. You only heard what you expected." Kitty stomped over to the dresser and picked up an engraved silver mirror, shoving it into Ashley's hands. "Look at yourself. Can you honestly say you're unattractive? What is it about you that a man can't love?"

Ashley did as ordered, dabbing at her red-rimmed eyes. "It has nothing to do with my appearance."

"What, then?"

"I'm not sure—some missing feminine quality that draws the opposite sex." She brought the mirror closer and sucked in her bottom lip. "Fan, you, me—we all were born without whatever it is. Mother realized it, probably the first time she looked at me. She always knew I'd never make a match. Just like you."

Kitty didn't state the obvious, allowing Ashley to reach the conclusion on her own. "But you—" She slapped the coverlet. "You *did* make a match. What happened, Kitty, after all these years? Why did you suddenly change your mind about getting married?"

Her aunt stretched out, leaning against the headboard. "The first part is going to sound familiar. I grew up feeling like I didn't belong in my family. I never wanted to go to school at Ashley Hall, or make my debut at St. Cecilia's. I wanted to be a rebel like

Fan. Not that I could ever get used to neat bourbon or those vile little black cigars she puffed on."

Kitty echoed Ashley's laughter, then sobered. "Lord, I miss that old termagant." She picked at a glittery sequin on the bodice of her jumpsuit. "Right before she died, Fan informed me that I'd bought into a myth. Her words—'bought into.'"

"What did she mean?" Ashley asked, recalling Michael saying that the world was full of myths and each person had to decide which ones to believe.

"She told me not to make the same mistake she did. That there's no substitute for building and sharing a life with one special person." Kitty smiled in bittersweet recollection. "Actually, she said, 'Girl, get yourself some passionate memories to warm you when you're old like I am. It's a bummer knowing I'm going to die without them.'"

Ashley's throat constricted. All at once, so many explosions were rocking her, eroding the foundations of her life. Now there was evidence that she had choices she'd always believed denied her. "Did Fan regret any of what she *had* done?"

"No, not at all. Her only regret was living alone for so long. She didn't want me to make the same mistake. After our talk, I started to look at things differently."

"Then you met Richard."

"And fell quite recklessly in love," Kitty added, beaming at Ashley. "I know most people probably find it amusing that this happened to me at my age, but I don't care. I can't imagine believing my life was full before Richard."

For the first time ever, Ashley saw a vulnerability in her aunt. Maybe love brought forth all sorts of hidden traits and emotions. When she spoke she was teary—not from sadness. "I find it perfectly romantic, and I'm happy because you're happy. Visibly so, I might add."

"Deliriously so. Does that tell you anything, my darling niece?"

Ashley opened her mind to the exciting, limitless possibilities. A renegade current of sensual awareness vibrated inside her. "I can do it, too, can't I, Kitty? I can have Michael. That is, if I'm woman enough to go after him, to take what I want."

"Well, are you?"

Ashley patted her chest, over her heart. "Am I ever. When I'm finished with him..." Her words trailed off as she rummaged in the nightstand drawer for something to write on and began scribbling a list. "I have to do this up big, so he'll have no doubt that I love him."

SIX DAYS LATER, Ashley collapsed into her window seat only moments before takeoff. She heaved a great sigh of relief and watched Atlanta disappear beneath her. She'd enjoyed the city she had called home for three years, but there were no regrets. She had a new home waiting for her—she hoped.

Accepting a soft drink from the attendant, Ashley thought back on her frantic activities of the past few days. She couldn't believe how cooperative everyone had been. Her MG was in storage at George's until she could drive it to Minnesota, and the apartment was up for sublease. Her boss had given her an indefinite leave of absence after Ashley agreed to fill in when nobody else was available for an audit. In less than a year, she'd be free of contractual obligations—able to do whatever pleased her. Or maybe by then she and Michael would be ready to start a family. She knew what kind of parent she wanted to be and was certain Michael would make an excellent father. He'd already taught her everything about love.

Ashley had even effected a truce of sorts with her mother. Sometime before he left, Michael had cornered Eleanor and set her straight about his feelings for Ashley. At the same time, he accused Eleanor of being responsible for her daughter's inability to accept those feelings, of making her feel unworthy of love.

Ashley smiled as she pictured that confrontation. Eleanor had been impressed, and contrite. Saturday, before Ashley left Charleston, her mother had made excuses and apologized after a fashion. Ashley had been magnanimous. By that time, she'd mapped out a whole new future—one that made her too happy to hold grudges, especially when she had more promising things beckoning.

THE LONGER HE LOOKED at the framed photo of the woman with the violets, the lower he felt. Michael swiveled his chair around and squinted out through the slatted blinds of his office window. Everyone else had gone and he ought to leave too. He couldn't summon up the energy to move. He watched a mallard duck family diving for food on the small lake behind the building. Wildlife in the middle of a city had always appealed to him, but now he found no pleasure in the sight.

He'd been sure today would be better, that he'd be able to concentrate on all the work he had ignored. Tomorrow it would be a week since he'd left Charleston, and the time had dragged by like no other week in memory.

"Damn it all!" he cursed and hammered his fist on the chair arm. He should have known better than to issue that ultimatum, even though Kitty had agreed it was his only recourse. It had given Ashley the opening to do what she'd planned all along—go back to her comfortable life and leave him behind.

Maybe he'd drive to the lake for the weekend. Pick up some Scotch and tie one on so he could really suffer and get it out of his system. He propped his heels on the sill and grimaced at the thought. Diving into a bottle wouldn't make him forget, and remembering their time together would be too painful.

Preoccupied, he didn't hear the door open.

Ashley stepped into the office, aware that she'd never crossed a more important threshold. Michael was facing the exterior wall and she waited quietly for him to turn around. The wait stretched on so long she feared he was asleep. But no, his pencil tapped steadily against the chair arm. Finally, the chair rotated and their eyes met.

"Returning to the scene of the crime, Ash?"

"I prefer to think of it as returning to where it all began."

"The only thing I need to know is if anything has changed since last Saturday night in Charleston."

Ashley's heartbeat kicked into double time. She tossed the airline ticket onto his desk. "How about this for starters?" She watched him hold the folder. A slight frown creased his forehead, but she'd expected that.

He placed it in front of him and said, "I guess I'm dense, but I don't know what this means."

"Open it!" He did, and found two airline tickets, one for Michael Jordan, one for Ashley A. Jordan. Round trips from Las Vegas to Tahiti and back to Minneapolis.

"Nevada," she explained softly. "Marriage with no waiting period."

The merest hint of a smile flirted at the corners of his mouth. Ashley dropped into the nearest chair, fearing her knees would fail her.

"Are you proposing, Ashley?"

"You already did that. I'm attending to details. It's what I'm good at, you know." She kept her eyes on the tickets, refusing to let his silence eat away at her confidence. "Will you be on that flight next Friday?"

"Are you sure this is what you want?"

"I've never considered myself a gambling woman." How could she sound so cool when her insides were churning like a washing machine?

Michael regarded her for a long time before he nodded. Still he didn't say anything.

Ashley shifted in the chair, determined that the next line would be his.

At last, the smile that had melted her heart, as well as her resistance, reached out to her across the space that separated them. "Aren't you forgetting something?"

"Like what?" She was bursting to tell him the most important part.

"The only thing that will make me get on that plane. The only thing that really matters."

Her smile rivaled his. "Michael, I love you. Completely and forever."

His eyes closed for a few seconds. When he spoke, his voice was taut with emotion. "I like the sound of those words. Still, I need a little more reassurance." He stood and held out his arms. "Come here, Ash."

She got up, but didn't take a step. "I've already come a lot further than I ever dreamed possible."

Michael started toward her. By the time he reached halfway, Ashley rushed into his embrace. After a long, satisfying kiss, she smiled up at him. "I couldn't wait. Think you can put up with that kind of impulsiveness on a permanent basis?"

"Why not? After all, that's the woman I first fell in love with."

Everyone loves a spring wedding, and this April,
Harlequin cordially invites you to read the most
romantic wedding book of the year.

ONE WEDDING—FOUR LOVE STORIES
FROM OUR MOST DISTINGUISHED
HARLEQUIN AUTHORS:

BETHANY CAMPBELL
BARBARA DELINSKY
BOBBY HUTCHINSON
ANN McALLISTER

*The church is booked, the reception arranged and the
invitations mailed. All Diane Bauer and Nick Granatelli
have to do is walk down the aisle. Little do they realize that
the most cherished day of their lives will spark so many
romantic notions....*

Available wherever Harlequin books are sold.

HARLEQUIN
American Romance®

THE ROMANCE THAT STARTED IT ALL!

For Diane Bauer and Nick Granatelli, the walk down the aisle was a rocky road....

Don't miss the romantic prequel to WITH THIS RING—

I THEE WED
BY ANNE McALLISTER

Harlequin American Romance #387

Let Anne McAllister take you to Cambridge, Massachusetts, to the night when an innocent blind date brought a reluctant Diane Bauer and Nick Granatelli together. For Diane, a smoldering attraction like theirs had only one fate, one future—marriage. The hard part, she learned, was convincing her intended....

Watch for Anne McAllister's I THEE WED, available *now* from Harlequin American Romance.

ITW